Kenerly

.

Kenerly

Kenerly

PAPERBACK VERSION

ISBN-13: 978-0615691459

ISBN-10: 0615691455

LCCN: 2012954047

Printed in the United States of America

Cover Design: Wayne Grace II

Cover Model: Beirzhette Amyre

Book Edited by: AMB Publishing Productions

ambpublishing@gmail.com

http://ambpublishingpr.blogspot.com

www.twitter.com/ambpublishingpr

http://urbanfictionnoveltreasure.blogspot.com

TREASURE

SHAUNTA KENERLY

INTRODUCTION

It is Saturday morning and I am out at the Easton mall with my girl Brandi doing some shopping. We try to hook up with each other at least once a week to have a girl's day. With our busy schedules, sometimes these days are far and few in. Normally every day I am with my brother Lamar, either making moves to drop off some dope to his many clients or plotting to get a rival hustler. He and I have been setting people up for about two years now. I must say that I do like manipulating a man's mind and then robbing him for everything he has not leaving a trace of my whereabouts. I am living a good life. I do like making the quick money when we do the drop-offs, but I much rather take a man's money after putting in the time and giving myself to him. Lamar watches each one of my licks carefully making sure that he has enough money for us to take. I enjoy being the "show girl" for my licks to show off for his boys and spend money on. I never catch feelings for a target or let them get close to me. Lamar has warned me that when I catch feelings for a target that is when I will let my guard down and my life will be in jeopardy. Although some of these men are very well off, damn handsome, drive European cars, dress nice, and treat me very well. I have to keep it strictly business.

Walking out of the shoe store with three boxes of heels, I attempt to cross the street heading for the lingerie store but my cell phone suddenly rings. I answer the call quickly seeing that the caller is my brother. Lamar tells me that he needs me to meet him at my apartment so I can ride with him and his boys to meet a new customer, here in Columbus. Brandi overhears my conversation and her body language shows her attitude. Lamar tells me that I can make

$1,500 just walking in the place with him. I am not hurting for money but after spending $500 on heels and another $300 on a pair of glasses, a bitch needs to get paid. I jump at the opportunity and tell him that I will be in the house before he gets off the highway.

Lamar picks me up in his brand-new candy painted blue Range Rover with his best friend Scotty in the back. I ask why he did not tell me about this job yesterday and he claims that it just came up. The person whom we are going to meet knows another crew that Lamar deals with. The crew had said that the guy wasn't wanting anything too big because he mainly focuses on his legitimate businesses but keeps a few bricks of cocaine in the streets. Hearing that I knew that this was not somebody my brother wanted me to introduce myself to and possibly rob. We only focused our attention on men who had bricks on deck themselves and was moving a lot of weight.

We arrive at our meeting location, on the east side of Columbus. I am stunned to see that we are meeting a drug dealer at a hair and nail shop. Lamar reads my face and bust out laughing. He and I exit the truck walking inside of the shop leaving Scotty behind to watch our backs. When we enter, all of the employees stop and stare along with some of the customers. I smile at the attention and walk directly towards the owner's office. Lamar steps in front of me gripping one hand on the duffel bag and the other hand on his pistol. I do not know if I should pull my little 380 out or take a seat to get a fill in. Lamar allows me to get around him so that he can close the door behind us. At the office desk sits this fine ass light-skinned brother with waves swirling around his head as if he was on a hair box. His muscular build showed through his V- neck T-shirt. He quickly ends his call and embraces my brother with a manly hug. I study his body very well believing that he reminds me of the R&B singer and producer Tank. The only difference between the two is that you can see his thug swagger. I take a seat on the soft leather sofa and imagine him and me in my bed making love in every position. I catch myself closing my eyes tighter and rubbing my thighs. Lamar breaks my concentration shoving my shoulder telling me that it is time to leave. Time went by so fast that all I remember was Lamar bustin' open a brick for him to taste. Before I could stand to my feet, the man rushed over to me and begged to allow him to assist me. I am amazed by his actions, not ever knowing a man to be a thug and a gentleman. His actions took me by such a surprise that I cannot resist but smile. He does not hesitate to complement me on my beauty and smile.

Lamar laughs once again but takes no time to leave for the truck. I try to speed walk behind Lamar but I am being cautious not to fall in these heels. The last thing I want is to make a fool of myself in front of him and a crowd of jealous bitches. He stays right behind me step by step. I purposely sway my hips so that he can take notice at my luscious curves. Just before I reach the door, he asks me to stop and talk to him. I wonder what took him so long. I wanted him to stop me in front of everyone so they can really have something to look at. I turn to him trying to resist from smiling again but I cannot. Here I am twenty-six years old and I am acting as if I am in high school again.

"Can I get your name?" he said politely.

"Yes you may. My name is Treasure." I said like a schoolgirl.

"Treasure, that is a beautiful name for such a beautiful woman."

"Thank you." I reply.

"Well, I don't ever mix business with pleasure but I have to be able to take you out. I know that I don't look like much right now but I wasn't expecting to see someone as beautiful as you today."

His words surprise me. I have a loss for words. I pull out my cell phone and ask for his number so that I can call him. He saves my number and tells me that his name is Rashad.

Chapter 1

Five years has passed since the day I met Rashad. We dated for six months until he decided to propose to me and take me away from my unstable life. Rashad and I got married and a few months later, we had a son named Raymond. Rashad and I are the perfect couple and our family and friends envy us. Rashad continues to do business with my brother allowing me to be a stay-at-home mom. I promise Rashad that I would not ever again turn back to my old life. After months of being secretive, I told him how I make my real money taking men by surprise. He assured me that I would never have to want for anything and loving him would be enough for us.

Rashad being my husband, I listen to him before anyone. Lamar tries to catch me off guard testing me with potential licks but he knows that I will never dare to go against my husband's wishes. Because of this, I have separated myself from my brother causing some friction at times with my family. The relationship between my brother and I has disintegrated. Lamar's only care is for his nephew. Rashad takes notice at Lamar's comments but never utters a word. He reminds me of the dangerous life I had before I met him and I understand his every word. The only thing I do not agree with is that he tries to keep my mother from seeing Raymond. My mother is a Christian woman and loves her only grandchild to death. She tries to volunteer her time to baby-sit Raymond, but Rashad always objects hurting my mother's feelings. She does not share her feelings with Lamar, not knowing what he will do to Rashad. Rashad claims that it is too much for either of us to travel on the highway from Columbus to Dayton just to take Raymond to visit her. I am torn.

Business with Lamar and Rashad has grown so much that Rashad barely has time to oversee the beauty shop. I have since taken over the responsibilities of the shop, in order to allow him to serve the Columbus streets. Over the years, Rashad has gained trust with my brother, which is hard to do. Lamar has begun to deliver extra weight with Rashad fronting him until the next time they meet. With all of this weight coming in, Rashad asks for his cousin Malik and some of his old friends he played college football with to, help distribute, creating their own team of hustlers.

Becoming so busy with business around the city and small towns nearby, Rashad allows one of his boys to travel alone to Louisville, Kentucky to take one of his client's two bricks of heroin and three bricks of cocaine. Rashad's friend was trying to rush down there and back to get paid and a Kentucky State police officer pulled him over for speeding finding all of the drugs. He was detained and called Rashad informing him of the news and pleaded to Rashad for a lawyer. Rashad acted fast with calling a defense lawyer that is known to beat cases in Louisville but this case is open and shut. After talking with the lawyer, Rashad calls Lamar and tries to explain the situation to him but Lamar does not understand excuses. He just wants his money or his shit back.

With the security and power of his crew, Rashad begins to feel himself and tells Lamar to forget about it or do what he has to do. Those words do not sit well with Lamar. My brother's crew is made up of niggas who are really out here taking federal life chances and do not care and will kill anyone in their way. Just two years ago, Scotty beat a double homicide charge and the trial did not affect the way he handled his business. Lamar is not just protected by his boys, but by their supplier, some crazy Haitians in Cincinnati.

Lamar calls me on the office phone after trying to call me numerous times on my cell phone but I was unable to answer trying to finish the count for the day. I answer already disturbed, but Lamar quickly gets to the point. He tells me that Rashad owes him money and he needs it now. Besides owing Lamar, Rashad had the balls to talk shit to Lamar knowing that my brother is nuts. Tears suddenly fall down my face with the thought of what my brother has in mind for him. I plead with Lamar to give me some time to talk to Rashad, but Lamar tells me that he has heard enough. He is only calling to warn me to stay away from him. Lamar stresses that he did not want me in the way when he handles Rashad.

Ending my call with Lamar, I immediately call Rashad rushing out of the shop. Crying hysterically over the phone, I try to warn Rashad about Lamar as if he did not know. I tell him that I respect and love him but this amount of money was not something to play with. He brags on how tough he and his crew are, but he does not understand how deep my brother is. I have seen with my own eyes how mad my brother gets when someone tests him. All of the situations were ended with a bullet. Rashad shouts at me believing that I am siding with my brother and disrespecting his crew then he hangs the phone up on me. I try calling repeatedly, but I do not get an answer.

Arriving at home, I notice that his car is not in the garage. I took Raymond over to Brandi's house after I leave the shop, so just in case some shit was to go down, I do not want him around. Brandi does not question why I am in such a rush to get home, but allows me to leave without saying a word. Watching the garage door close, I decide to lock it also. I am shaking uncontrollably from the nervousness. My mind is racing with so many thoughts. I pour myself a tall glass of wine, almost drinking the whole bottle in no time. Rashad finally calls me back and after hearing the urgency in my voice, assures me that he will be home soon. He claims he just has one more client to meet. My nerves calm down a little knowing that he will be home soon.

I call Brandi and tell her about what is going on and she does not take the news by surprise. Brandi states that she has noticed Rashad feeling himself more lately. Brandi also claims that Rashad's name is echoing in the streets, getting all of his private matters in the street. Instead of being the low-key businessman, he has become known as a hustler. She does not like Rashad much, so she quickly stood firm defending Lamar. I have to remind her that he is my husband and my son's father. Brandi knows this, but reminds me that he chose this lifestyle. We talk for thirty more minutes until Rashad finally enters the house.

Rashad opens the door smiling showing all of his teeth. I have been home crying my eyes out anticipating for him to arrive home safe and he has the audacity to stroll in here like he does not have a care in the world. For some reason his smile pisses me off. I violently throw my glass in his direction barely missing him and causing the glass to explode against the wall.

"What the fuck is wrong with you!" Rashad shouts.

I stand on my feet, "What the fuck is wrong with

12

me? You walk in here as if you do not have a price on your head. Do you care about your life? Shit do you care about your wife and your son? We need you!" I scream causing my voice to break.

Rashad grabs my arms looking at me with his brown eyes. "You don't have to worry about me. I am not going anywhere! No one is going to do shit to me!"

"How can you be so sure? Did you and my brother work things out? Because if you did not, trust me he will do something to you." I cry.

"Your brother doesn't want to fuck me. He knows where to find me. So if he wanted to get his damn money, he could have tried to come and get it! Fuck your brother and his niggas! Rashad exclaims.

"I can't imagine something happening to you. We will be left all alone." I say walking away from him.

"I will always be here. You do not have to worry about that. Look, I am home now."

I walk back to him smiling from ear to ear. He always had a way with his words to make me feel better. Locked in his tight hug, we passionately kiss each other. Rashad picks me up and carries me to the bedroom.

He gently lays me across the pillow-soft bed and begins to take off his clothes. The sight of my man's physique makes my pussy pulsate for what is to come. He slowly undresses me, and I am enjoying his touch. Down to my lace panties, he smiles at me and begins to kiss my inner thigh. I slowly spread my legs open giving him the green light to do whatever he wants. Rashad accepts my invitation, and slides my panties off with ease. He climbs on top of me and begins to scroll his tongue over my nipples simultaneously massaging my breast. His touch is causing my pussy to become soaking wet with my natural nectar. Rashad continues to scroll his tongue over my body slowly creeping down in between my thighs tasting all of me.

We make love to each other over an hour until he becomes exhausted. I admit, I did wear him out when I climbed on top and continued to ride him until I was satisfied.

As we lay next to each other, I feel a sense of relief knowing that he is safe next to me. I stare through the window wondering when Rashad will decide to give up this life and be a real husband for me. I would like to have him lying next to me every night but when you live his life these nights are few and far in between. I fall asleep dreaming of the life we could have.

Suddenly I am awaken by a strange noise. I sit up anticipating another noise. I look over at Rashad and he is sleeping like a baby. As bad as I want to wake him I decide against it. I believe that the sound might have been Raymond tossing in his bed. I stare at the door waiting to see if he will walk in but the door remains shut. I remember the sound being loud but distant from our bedrooms. Next, I remember that Raymond is at Brandi's. Becoming nervous, I shake Rashad until he is awakened.

"Rashad get up, I just heard something coming from down stairs."

"T, go back to bed you are tripping." Rashad replies with a groggy voice.

"No I'm not!" I stress.

"Maybe you heard a car door or somebody riding pass blasting their music."

I slide back down under the covers. "Yeah, you might be right."

"I am always right," he chuckles.

Soon as I become comfortable and stry to go back to sleep, the sound re-enters my mind. I decide to wake up and check for myself without disturbing him. I open my eyes slowly and see two men standing at the foot of my bed with guns in their hands. Quickly a gloved hand covers my mouth keeping me from screaming. I do not want to squirm in the bed not knowing what these men would do to me. I barely turn my head, look from the corner of my eye, and see that the gloved man is Scotty. "Oh shit!" I muffle. Scotty slowly takes away his hand from my mouth and signals for me to be quiet. I look over at Rashad and my brother is standing over him quietly cocking back his gun. I try to stare at Lamar with pleading eyes but he does not pay me any attention. The look on my brother's face is a look that I have seen on numerous occasions, right before someone feels his rage. My chest tightens and I instantly begin to shed tears. I believe that this might be the last night that I would be lying next to Rashad. Lamar forcefully punches Rashad in the face causing him to wake up with disbelief written all over his face. He looks Lamar in his eyes, seeing the killer before him. Rashad flops around the bed like a fish out of water trying to escape Lamar's aim. Lamar slaps him to the face with the gun handle causing Rashad's nose to burst wide open. Rashad yells out in agony holding his bloody nose.

15

Lamar leans over and places the gun easily inside of Rashad's mouth.

"You did not think that I had forgotten about you, did you?" Lamar asks provokingly.

Rashad tries to hold back any signs of fear but Lamar has a sixth sense for knowing when someone fears him. Lamar grabs Rashad by the neck forcing him to gag on the pistol.

"Listen here you bitch ass nigga, I want you to get my muthafucking money tonight or you will not live to see tomorrow. You need to get on the phone and tell your bitch ass cousin to get me my shit within the next hour or he will be using the money to burry your ass!"

One of the men standing at the foot of the bed steps out of shadows, handing Rashad his cell phone. Rashad quickly takes the phone and calls Malik.

I hear the nervousness in his voice as he gives Malik instructions where to pick up some money around the city. Malik must also notice the nervousness in his voice because he continues to question why should he get up from his bed to get the money. Rashad becomes aggravated, and shouts his orders again receiving Malik's full attention. Lamar and his boys laugh at his actions.

"Yeah nigga, talk that gangster shit to him," Lamar chuckles.

Rashad ends his call, "He will have the money gathered up soon. Do you want him to bring it here?"
"I should say fuck the money and kill your stupid

ass and the rest of your niggas."

"No, no, don't do that man!" Rashad pleads.

"You think I do this shit for fun nigga? You owe me so one way or another you have to pay. You call your cousin back and tell him to meet my boys at your shop on Cleveland Avenue. You already know what will happen to you if the money is short or they try to do some silly shit. Nigga I will kill you, your cousin, and the rest of your soft ass niggas!" Lamar said meaning every word.

Rashad did not hesitate to call Malik and warn him not to try Lamar. Overhearing the conversation, Malik does not want to look like a punk by giving in to Lamar's demands. Rashad has to philosophize to him for a moment about the game. Reminding him that when you take chances, you take a chance at taking a loss. This was their loss. He tells Malik that they will be able to make up the loss in no time. Again, he instructs him, but reminding him that time is of the essence.

After ending the call, Lamar snatches Rashad out of the bed and forces him downstairs. I let out a loud cry receiving my brother's attention. He looks at me with disgust and shakes his head. I sit alone crying hard imagining what will happen to Rashad. Feeling a breeze of cold air, I notice that I am sitting in the bed naked for my brother and his friends to see. I take the bed sheet from the bed and follow them down stairs.

Lamar forces Rashad down on the couch, keeping a steady aim on him. The man I call my husband is crying like a woman. My brother has instilled so much fear into him that every time he would try to speak he would fumble over his words. Scotty and the other two laugh at Rashad's actions but they knew Lamar could take their humor the wrong way and ignite.

Suddenly Lamar's cell phone rings, taking him away from his friends' laughter. He talks with the other people who meet Malik at the shop. I hear his tone of voice change telling me that the meeting went well. I feel a sense of relief and thank God under my breath.

Lamar ends his call and informs his crew that they have the money. Besides Lamar and Scotty, the other two rejoice. One of them speak up and asks Lamar if they can leave. Lamar hesitates but nods his hand in agreement. They slowly walk towards the door before leaving out.

I take this opportunity to sit next to Rashad for his protection.

"What is up with these young niggas these days man?" Lamar inquires looking for Scotty's response.

"I paid you now you can go." Rashad manages to say softly.

Lamar becomes upset and again waives his gun in Rashad's face. Rashad clenches onto my waist pulling me closer.

"Nigga, you think that my sister is saving your bitch ass? Don't let your dumb ass thinking get you killed! Because, if it was not for my nephew, I would have gotten your ass a long time ago. So from now on, every day you look at him, thank him because he is the reason why you are still breathing. Do you understand that?"

"Yeah. Yeah I got you."

"Treasure, why in the hell did you marry this bitch ass nigga? You have more balls than he do."

I sit quietly staring at my brother not knowing if I should respond. Luckily, Scotty tells him that they should leave so that they can get the money back to Christian.

Christian is the brains of my brother's crew. He handles all communication between their crew and the Haitians. He keeps account of every gram being sold and every dollar being count.

"Alright I am out. If I hear that you are not being a man for my sister or a father to my nephew I will not think twice about killing you!" Lamar said sternly walking out the door.

Chapter 2

Rashad and Lamar stopped doing business with each other since the day Lamar had to threaten him. It has been two months since then, and it has been dreadful for me. Rashad has been all up under me watching my every move. It has been weeks since Brandi and I had a chance to go shopping. Rashad has been depressed not taking care of his appearance and moping around the house. Now having the only income coming from the shop it is hard for us to live our normal life. Rashad has changed into another person whom I do not recognize. He has become a paranoid wreck. He believes that I will leave him for some other man although he stays up under me 24/7. It is sad to see him like this. Every day we argue either at home or at the shop because of his jealousy or daily drinking. Not able to spend time with his friends in the streets getting money, he uses that time to buy alcohol and stay drunk. It is hard for me to stick by his side watching him become a stranger to his son and me. Raymond has become scared of his father, not knowing if he will yell at him or hug him at times. Every time I try to discuss our problems, it turns into an argument. I just try to stay away from him and ignore his ass, but most of the time that does not help the situation. If my mother did not raise me to stick out the rough times ahead in a relationship, I would have left by now. Luckily, Rashad's friend who made the pros knew of a connect down in Atlanta who would be able to supply Rashad and his boys with whatever they wanted. When he received that news, the hustler I have known for so many years appeared and the insane nut vanished. Rashad gets himself all cleaned up and is quick to share the news with Malik.

Malik on the other hand managed to keep his sanity and his hustler's spirit alive. He had put away a few bricks for hard times like these. There were always times when either the prices went up or the supply was hard to find. Malik and Rashad did not have a problem finding the dope it was that they messed with Lamar for so long that they did not have anyone else to buy good quality dope from. Malik managed to keep money in his pockets by stretching his product out to the last gram.

When Rashad called Malik about the news, they were both acting as if one of their cousins came home from doing a stretch behind bars. Rashad discusses the plans with Malik and he is ready.

Rashad and the rest of his boys get together at our house and discuss business about their future connect. They all enter the house with duffle bags of money to buy the dope with, throwing all of the bags on my sofa. I want to snap on their manners, but decide against it, knowing that my husband is about to go to work.

The very next day Malik, Rashad and another member of his team take the trip down with hopes of bringing back some good dope to supply the streets. Rashad is very excited but that does not distract him from being cautious and taking his pistol with extra ammunition.

Chapter 3

Rashad and Malik have been making monthly trips down to Atlanta, proving to be very profitable. After making the profit off their first trip, Rashad goes and buys us matching BMWs for our anniversary. Rashad is back to his old loving self and things are back to the way they used to be before his breakdown.

Today at the shop Rashad calls me asking that I rush home. At first, I object knowing that today is the beginning of the month and it is Saturday. I want to get all of the money that I can from the shop. The beginning of the month was a huge pay day and I always look forward to it. I have ways to encourage clients to get both their hair and nails done all in one stop. The tone in Rashad's voice signales for me to reframe from arguing and find out what my man needs me for.

I enter the house and notice that Rashad has his luggage and duffle bags near the door. I figure that he is prepared to go on his trip but what is out of the ordinary is my suitcase also near the door. I wonder why he has my suitcase out like he is taking it also.

"Are we going somewhere?" I question.

"Malik has to take care of some important business, so he will not be able to take the trip with me down the way. You and he are the only two people that I can trust with this." Rashad announce sadly.

"So you want me to go with you?"

"Yes T." He says reluctantly.

I am happy to get away from Columbus for a while and enjoy myself alone with my husband. Rashad has already made plans for Raymond to stay over at Brandi's and has even dropped him off. I finish packing the things I like and we hit the interstate.

When we arrive at the hotel in downtown Atlanta, a beautiful host greets us with a pretty smile and wonderful hospitality. Rashad and Malik have been staying here the last few trips so the host already recognizes Rashad. I assume that he has flirted with her every time. Rashad and her share some small talk and laughter before he formally introduce me.

"Hi, my name is Kyra. Call down if you need anything."

"Thank you. I will keep that in mind."

She hands over to Rashad our room key cards but I cannot help but notice her beauty. I wonder to myself why a woman as beautiful as she is would be working here. She should be a model or in somebody's video. Staring at her body and facial features, I know that she is from Latin ethnicity. I catch her staring back at me ignoring whatever Rashad has to say to her. She has this weird look on her face as if she is wondering about me also.

We say our goodbye's and head for the elevator. Right before the door opens, she runs over to me and hands me a flyer to a lounge. Kyra says that the lounge is nearby and that it is very nice inside. She reads my mind knowing that I would like to get out and enjoy the time here. Kyra suggest to Rashad to take me to the lounge to have a good time. Rashad brushes off the idea but not so much for her feelings to be hurt. I thank her for trying to help the situation and placed the flyer in my purse.

Rashad and I enter the room setting aside our luggage. He carefully places the bag of money underneath the bed and places his pistol on top of the night stand. Rashad tells me to get comfortable, as he undress flopping down on the king sized bed. I ignore him and walk throughout the room to do a detailed inspection. At the end of my inspection, Rashad is damn near sleep watching a college football game. I become instantly aggravated with him knowing that I wanted to do some shopping or just view the city. This is our first time going out of town since before Raymond was born. I am always stuck in the house or at the shop. When he does remember that I am his wife, we only go out to eat or go to the movies. I stare at him with disbelief as he is all sprawled out in his boxers and muscle shirt.

"What are you doing Rashad?"

He turns on his side away from me, "T, I am tired. I drove all of the way here. Let me get a few hours of sleep and then we can do whatever you want."

"Rashad I am not going to sit here in this hotel staring at the television!" I snap.

"Look I am tired and I am going to get some sleep. If you don't understand that then I do not know what to tell you. You can take the car and do whatever. I will be here when you get back. The keys are by the door."

I stomp over to get the keys and slam the door

behind me. I do not know where I am going, I just know that I have to get away from him right now.

Getting off of the elevator I continue my pace rapidly walking through the lobby slapping my heels against the marble floor. I take notice at Kyra sitting alone reading an urban magazine. She sits quietly reading on a love-seat with her golden legs crossed over another. I momentarily stand in front of her studying her sexy legs up her thick thighs. Her business skirt showed confidence and class. Kyra's long black hair laid over her breast which magnetically gravatated my eyes to her cleavage. She pulls away the magazine and glances up at me noticing my pressence.

"Kyra is it?" I ask knowingly.

"Yes."

"Maybe when you get off you can show me how to get to the club. I would like to get a quick drink and enjoy some music."

"Well if you can wait for about twenty minutes, I will go with you. I am waiting for another manager to relieve me." Kyra says.

"Yes, I can wait. That will not be a problem. Thanks girl. I do not want to sit up in that room with my boring ass husband all weekend."

"I understand that but that is a man for you girl. Let me go grab my things so that when the manager shows up you can follow me. Is it alright if I go home to change first? I have to get out of these work clothes."

"That will be fine." I cheerfully say.

I wait for Kyra outside of her urban Atlanta apartment. Not familiar with the area I am constantly studying my surroundings. Being raised in a bad area I know what can happen to someone in a split second. I am comfortable waiting for her but one can never be too careful.

Minutes later, Kyra exits her apartment wearing a pair of fitted designer jeans, stiletto heels, a casual blouse which continues to show off her full size breast, and some jewelry. Oddly I become attracted to her in a trance like state as she walks towards the car. My eyes take in every curve her body has to offer. I have to admit she looks better now than before.

Inside of the lounge, we are drinking glasses of wine sharing multiple conversations. I feel so comfortable with her that I share my personal life with her. Sharing stories I come to find out how much we have in common. I found out that her family is from the Dominican Republic, and that is where she gets her accent and figure.

Continuing to shainsert-sore our conversation, suddenly a song is played by the DJ that reminds me of Rashad. The song is from the artist Tank. I close my eyes and listen to the lyrics carefully. Not being able to sit still, I stand to my feet and imagine myself dancing with my husband. Kyra stands up dancing also and singing along with the lyrics. I laugh at her but quickly zone back into the music. I imagine Rashad's and my first time slow dancing at a lounge, sort of like this one. I put my imagination to the test and imagine us dancing in front of our family and friends at our wedding. With my eyes tightly close I can fell Kyra pull on my hands and begin to dance with me when the chorus comes on. She steps closer to me looking at me like she did when I saw her behind the desk. Kyra takes my hands and gently place them on her apple shaped ass. I am surprised by her actions but my hands do not move. She takes this opportunity to come closer having our breast touching and sucks the lip gloss off my bottom lip. Her lips are unbelievably soft that I cannot resist but to kiss her back. We share kisses until the song end.

After the song we separate but continuing to stare at each other. Kyra take a sip from her glass but does not take her eyes from me. I sit motionless with multiple emotions running through my body. I take my eyes away from her trying to get myself together. My cell phone begins to chime bringing myself back to reality. I quickly search for my phone in my purse remembering that Brandi has my son and I have not talked to her since Rashad and I were on the interstate. When I answer I become at ease knowing that the caller is Rashad. I look away from Kyra trying to act as if she is not there. I do not want him to think that I am out doing anything for us to get into an argument over.

"Hi baby." I cheerfully say.

"What's up baby? Are you done with your shopping?"

I turn back at Kyra before speaking, "I'm not out shopping. I am out with a friend."

"A friend! You don't know anybody down here."

"You don't know who I know. I am out with my friend Kyra." I state sarcastically.

Kyra hears my conversation and playfully blows me a kiss. I smile as chills run up my body. I am anticipating the next time I will taste her lips again.

"Kyra who works here at the hotel?" He says surprised.

"Yes Rashad."

"Shit, what are y'all doing that I couldn't be a part of?"

"Remember Mr. Sleepy that you wanted to stay in the room and sleep. Well I found someone who did not mind entertaining me. "

When those words rolled off my tongue, Kyra seductively licked her lips at me and slid her hands between her thighs. I move the phone away from my mouth and whisper for her to stop playfully before Rashad suspects me of something. Kyra ignores my pleas and playfully flirts.

"Well, how about we all go out to eat. I know of a nice bar and grill place that we will be able to enjoy ourselves at. I woke up hungrier than a muthafucka."

"I will ask her but I do not know if she will feel comfortable going out with us."

"Yes I will go Rashad!" Kyra says loud enough for him to hear.

"There it is then T. I will see y'all in a few." Rashad says ending our call.

We finish off our wine and leave the lounge heading for the hotel.

Sitting outside of the hotel, I try calling Rashad numerous times without receiving an answer, Kyra suggests that we go in and check on him. She says that he may have gone back to sleep.

Opening the door of our hotel room I look around and Rashad is not anywhere in sight. I notice that he has his designer suit and loafers lying on the bed ready to be worn. I snuck this suit in his suitcase just in case we decided to go somewhere fancy. I have a bad ass designer dress to match his perfectly. Not wasting any time I quickly undress in front of Kyra and toss my clothes onto the bed where I notice Rashad's phone. I pick up his phone with disgust knowing why he was unable to answer my calls. Down to my panties and bra, I grab my things from out of my luggage and place the dress down next to his suit. As I quickly move about, I feel my 34D breast bouncing uncontrollably. I check behind me to see if Kyra remains in the room and she has her eyes glued on my every movement.

With my bra and panties in my hand, I rush over to the bathroom to take a quick shower. I want to be ready before Rashad decides to show up. I do not know where he has gone, but I'm not going to play my girl Kyra.

Snatching the bathroom door open aggressively, I am caught off guard from what I see. Rashad is standing in front of the mirror shaping up his neatly trimmed beard. Beads of water remain on his naked body dripping onto the floor as he carefully shaves. He glances over at me noticing my presence but quickly turns back to the mirror. Rashad's naked muscular body instantly excites me. Just the thought

29

of making love to him right now is driving me crazy knowing that Kyra is sitting a few feet away. I place my things down on the long double sink counter and skillfully pull my panties off without getting his attention. Within seconds I am totally naked but I keep my heels on for his delight. I step around him and slowly turn on the shower. With his back facing me, I gently place my hands on his broad shoulders and softly place kisses along his back and shoulders.

"What are you doing T? You know that we do not have time for this." He says as if I am bothering him.

"Shut up and let me handle this." I whisper into his ear seductively.

I slide my hands down his back lightly scratching him. I reach around his waist to stroke his shaft until he becomes hard. Rashad does not say a word allowing me to please him. He places the razor blade back inside of his grooming bag and wipes off the remaining cream. Getting his shaft to my approval, I turn him around by the waist and place all of him inside my mouth. I take him by total surprise almost causing him to lose his balance. If it was not for the counter he would have fell onto the floor. While I am teasing him by swirling my tongue over the tip of his shaft I pleasure myself with my fingers. I can feel Rashad growing larger and larger in my hand and as willing as I am to have every inch go inside of me, I decide against it because my fingers are doing a damn good job. I take my imagination off of me to open my eyes and see the look on his face. When I look up at him, his eyes are not on me, nor shut, but he is looking towards the door. I turn my head and notice that his attention is aimed at Kyra. Kyra is standing in the door way watching us as she undresses. She gives us a slow striptease but manages to keep eye contact with me. She removes all of her clothing revealing her perfect round breasts, toned stomach, and sexy ass tattoos. Kyra softly caresses her body getting my full attention. I remember how good our kiss was and wonder if she would like to demonstrate her talents on Rashad's shaft. I openly invite her to join us. She quickly squats down while she stays in her heels and assisst me. Rashad and I have not ever experienced a threesome before, but tonight will change that. I want Kyra more than Rashad can imagine. Rashad braces himself against the counter and allows us to share his shaft. Kyra and I take brief breaks sharing his shaft to give each other some attention. I can't resist her touch. She simultaneously pleases Rashad with her tongue and runs her finger all over my wet pussy. Her touch feels so good and by the look on Rashad's face I know that he loves her special talents. I allow her to take control while I stand up to exchange kisses with him. He grabs my ass squeezing it firmly. I am so turned on by his grasp that I spread my legs open so that he can feel my wetness. I ease his hand down my body and before his hand reaches my wetness Kyra stops him. She takes his hand and places it on her head as she tastes the both of us. As bad as I want to give my man my attention I cannot. Kyra has the perfect touch which is driving me crazy. Rashad tightens his grasp and rushes to suck on my breast signaling that he is ready to have an orgasm.

"Rashad I want to make love to you right now." I whisper in his ear.

Rashad positions himself to make love to me doggy-style which causes Kyra to move out the way. He forcefully drives his shaft inside me like never before. Kyra stretches out on the counter and slowly swirls her fingers inside of her moist pussy. I can hear the wetness clear as day.

Rashad also stares at Kyra thrusting harder watching her please herself. He grabs me by the waist and begins to grind until I feel him shoot inside me. I am pleased that he had an orgasm but I am not anywhere near finished. Just watching Kyra pleasure herself is teasing me. Rashad pulls away from me and I begin to inch closer towards Kyra. Kyra openly invites me, spreading her legs further apart. She places one foot on the counter for easy access. I smile at her gesure, but do not hesitate to taste her juices. I spread her lips open with my tongue getting myself a good taste before I went directly for her clit. I look behind me and Rashad is stroking himself hard again. I giggle from his actions but he is quickly ignored. For this to be my first time tasting another woman I have to admit that she does taste damn good. I keep my attention on her clit rapidly flicking my tongue causing her to have multiple orgasms. Rashad notices that we are enjoying each other's company so he decides to participate by placing himself back inside me.

Minutes later, I suggest that we all take a shower together to clean off. The shower is large enough to fit at least six people but tonight's maximum capacity will be three. Once inside the shower, Kyra and I lather each other and passionately kiss. Kyra and I are so much into one another that I yet again forget about Rashad. I occasionally feel him trying to touch me or notice his hands on Kyra. I do not understand why I don't become a bit jealous of his actions and continue to please Kyra. Rashad stands under the water with a sad look on his face. Being the down-ass wife that I always have been I signal for him to get a piece of Kyra himself. I carefully watch them while I keep myself moist. Rashad aggressively fucks Kyra placing her up against the wall. I quickly interrupt their festivities after a few strokes reminding Rashad that he needs to wear protection. Kyra agrees with me and squats down in front of

Rashad sucking the hell out of his dick until he lets out every drop he has to give. He looks at me with gratitude now smiling and shaking his head.

Kyra and I rapidly walk to the bed laughing like little girls. Catching me off guard, she pushes me down on the bed and looks at me with that weird look that I now recognize. I lay sprawled out studying her perfect measurements. Kyra gently spreads my yellow legs apart and caresses them firmly.

"Can I search for your treasure?" Kyra asks seductively with a strong island accent.

Biting down on my lips, I answer by shaking my head yes.

Skillfully she parts my legs and goes down head first between my thighs. Kyra swirls her tongue over my clit and thrusts her fingers inside of my soaking wet pussy. She has my thighs shaking like an earthquake. I am trying to resist, pulling the bed spread and squirming all over the bed. I grab hold onto a pillow and let out a loud screams as I squirt into her mouth. Rashad laugh at my actions and as bad as I want to throw something at him, I am paralyzed. Now each flicker has me jumping from the sensitivity. Rashad pulls away the pillow trying to stick his dick in my mouth but I forcefully push him away.

After handling her business with her tongue tasting all of my nectar she climbs on top of me and begins to suck on my nipples. I am so sensitive that my nipples can't take her tongue either. I don't want to tell her to stop ruining the moment, so I allow her to continue.

"Kyra do you have a condom?" Rashad interjects stroking his shaft.

Kyra looks up at me not knowing if she should answer, but I give her a blank look back wondering myself.

"Yes I do. They are in my purse. I will get them if it is okay with you." Kyra says waiting for my response.

"Go ahead and get them. I need a quick break in order to get myself together." I say waiving her to get her purse.

Kyra hops off the bed and quickly takes out three condoms from her purse. I watch her skillfully place the condom down his shaft.

"Take care of my man girl!" I shout playfully.

"Oh I will." Kyra says smiling at Rashad.

Kyra escorts Rashad to the bed and forcefully pushes him down on the bed causing me to flop. I get up from the bed so that I don't be a distraction and so that I can get a good visual. Kyra straddles Rashad slowly sliding his shaft into her. I catch her face screwing up from the pain but she does not frighten, continuing to get all of him inside her. Once he is all the way in Kyra starts to grind her ass against his thighs for a deeper penetration. Kyra slowly slides up and down his shaft with a nice rhythm. Each time she comes down her ass bounce off of his thighs causing a wave ripple to be showed on her ass. I get behind her and violently slap her ass to her delight. Kyra speeds up her pace managing to work her ass like a stripper trying to get paid. Suddenly my phone rings receiving all of my attention.

I rush over to answer the phone and notice that the caller is Brandi. I walk away from them because Kyra has now begun to make sensual loud noises and I do not want to tell Brandi all of the details. Her ass can get nosy at times. I enter the bathroom, closing the door behind me. Brandi is calling because Raymond wants to tell me good-night, which I thought was so sweet. I already miss my little man, I think to myself. Raymond and I talk briefly before we say our goodbyes. Brandi tells me what they have been doing so far today and their plans for tomorrow. Although she has my son and I am concerned about his welfare, I know that he is safe. I rush the conversation along so that I can entertain Kyra before my husband wears her out. Brandi catches me so she reluctantly ends the call.

I exit the bathroom and Kyra is now turned away from Rashad looking towards my direction rapidly bouncing her ass on him. Rashad is gripping onto her waist throwing her ass back down. Not wanting her to have all of the fun, I climb up on the bed and sit on his face allowing him to do something with his tongue. After a few minutes, Kyra and I agree on trading places for our pleasure. When I climb on top of him, I do not hesitate to take all of him inside me. He loves how wet my pussy feels letting out a moan. I work his shaft to my pleasure causing us to have an orgasm together. I open my eyes and see Kyra shaking uncontrollably having herself an orgasm in his mouth. I climb off him taking the condom to the bathroom. I look back and Rashad is eager for us to tag team him again. This is what I had to do to get some good loving from him?

Kyra and I again take turns sharing his dick until he hasbecome exhausted. After he decides to lye down to rest, he asks if he can watch us have sex. I am happy to hear that and want to show both of them what I can do.

CHAPTER 4

A month has passed since Rashad and I went
down to Atlanta to get his re-up. Today he is set to go back
down to meet with his connect. Malik has decided to come
today, so getting Rashad to ask me again to go with him
might be farfetched.

I rush home early today leaving the business of
the shop for one of my most trusted beautician's. I want to
catch Rashad at home before he is gone.

I have my bags packed and have them sitting
inside a closet which is near the front door. Knowing how
Rashad will act if I just come out with my bags, I decide
against it. I plan to persuade him by showing a little ass and
maybe even giving him some. I wait patiently on the bed
totally naked. I begin to caress my body with some body oil
imagining Kyra touching me. I slowly glide my hands over
my body causing myself to become moist. I take two of my
fingers and pleasure myself fantasizing about the whole
escapade. I swirl my fingers over my clit as if it was Kyra's
tongue. The thought of Kyra's tongue game is driving me
insane. I take a moment away from my clit and place my
fingers in my mouth, tasting my sweet nectar. I cannot wait
to see Kyra once again and hopefully we can get some time
alone. I thought that maybe while Rashad and Malik go off
to meet their connect, I could call Kyra to entertain me
again. Ever since I met her, I have not been able to get her
out of my head. Before taking the trip down there I would
not have ever thought of being with a woman and might
have smacked a bitch who would try to talk to me like that.

Rashad finally enters the house yelling at the top

of his lungs announcing his presence. I sit up in the bed waiting for him to walk through the bedroom door but he never enters. I hop up from the bed to find out what he is down there doing. When I get near the doorway I can hear him talking to someone. I figure that he is on the phone so I creep down to see who is so important that he cannot come up and make love to me. Stepping down a few stairs I am embarrassed to see Malik sitting at the bar counting money. I quickly cover my breast and rush back inside my room. Rashad bursts out laughing and tries to get Malik to laugh also, but he does not find the humor.

I allow some time to past before I threw some clothes on. After becoming fully dressed I walk downstairs and interrupt their conversation. Malik looks at me strangely but figures that it is time for him to leave. Rashad warns him to be here on time with the rental car. Malik understands, walking out the door. I am happy to hear that he doesn't plan to leave until the morning. I will have enough time to try to persuade him to take me.

Rashad tries to ignore my questions walking away from me drinking from his glass of vodka. He knows that I want to go with them but I am trying to get him to speak on it without me formally asking.

Entering our bedroom Rashad begins to pack his clothes ignoring my presence. I quickly undress and sprawl out over the bed waiting to capture his attention. When Rashad finishes packing, he looks at me with a smile shaking his head. I am wondering what is on his mind. I managed to keep my body glossed for his satisfaction.

"Rashad, where are you going?"

37

"I'm taking these bags downstairs so I will be ready in the morning."

"No. Set your bags down and come over here with your wife."

"T, what has gotten into you?" Rashad chuckles.

I sit up on and crawl across the bed to him. I grab him by his belt skillfully unbuckling his pants and placing his shaft inside my mouth. As I am sucking on the tip of his shaft I easily pull his pants to the floor. I quickly get his shaft to harden and obtain all of his attention. I crawl back to the top of the bed looking back at him with a seductive look. Rashad must be thinking that I am just messing with his head but I want to make sure that I get him in the palm of my hands. I begin to bounce my ass like a skilled stripper for his pleasure. Rashad is watching me stunned unable to say a word. I lye back on my decorative pillows and spread my legs apart as far as they can go. Rashad's eyes are as large as half dollars studying my flexibility. I slide my fingers inside stirring up my juices. Rashad becomes excited and quickly brings himself between my thighs tasting me. He samples my nectar just before throwing my legs on his shoulders and thrusting inside. With so much excitement he has an orgasm within a few strokes. I don't show him my disappointment but allow him to believe that I enjoyed it anyway. Knowing that I have to put on a show for him I give him about ten minutes to gather himself. I straddle him and kiss all over his chest and muscular stomach. Feeling his shaft stiffen, I grab it putting it back inside of me. I ride his shaft like I am auditioning for an adult film. Rashad tries to work back with me but I get him off rhythm in order to take control. I remembered how Kyra was working her ass on him and I stole some of her moves but continuing to do what I would normally do. Rashad is moaning and chanting for me to continue. Before I have another orgasm, I gently climb off.

"That's how you are going to play me?" Rashad questions becoming upset.

"Relax boy! I am going to take care of you." I said walking towards the dresserI decide to do what he has asked of me for years. I rub more oil over my legs and ass before I spread my ass open and lubricate it. I have always turned him down before believing that anal sex was only something white women would enjoy.

I stand alongside the bed and apply the oil down his shaft making sure that he is well lubricated before I stuck anything back there. Rashad is more than excited knowing what is to come. He aggressively grabs my ass and slaps it. I am nervous as hell but I am dedicated to do it for the trip. Rashad takes the bottle from my grasp and pour the oil down my back and over my ass again. He pulls me down to sit on his shaft gently easing it inside my backside. I allow myself to become at ease, carefully riding his shaft. After a few strokes, the pain disappears and turns into favorable pleasure. I manage to position myself so I really get into it and enjoy it. Rashad takes notice of me becoming more relaxed so he thrusts harder and faster. We both have an orgasm together causing us both to become fatigued. I lye there thinking that white women have been keeping this pleasure all to themselves.

I finally get up after lying down motionless. I wash my body very well before taking Rashad a warm washcloth so that I can do the same for him. I believe that while I have him well relaxed this will be my best opportunity to ask if I can go.

"Baby I have been wondering if I could go with you again, to Atlanta. We had so much fun." I say in a low tone.

"No, T. Malik and I are going down to get the shit and we are coming right back."

"I thought …" Rashad cuts me off.

"Look T, that was fun but it is back to business. I have to remain focused while I'm down there. You need to focus on taking care of our son and the shop. Damn, why did I give you the fucking shop if all you want to do is kick it?" Rashad questions me sarcastically.

"First of all, all I do is take care of my family and my home! The shop is bringing in more money now than it did when you were running it." I snap back.

"Fuck all of that! You are not going and that is it. You can be mad all you want but you are not coming." Rashad says pulling the covers over him.

Not wanting to continue the argument, I roll over pulling the comforter on top of me. Rashad tugs back but I maintain a tight grip. We do not say a word to the other and fall asleep.

CHAPTER 5

Today the shop is slow as hell on this cloudy afternoon. Maybe only ten customers have come in so far. I am bored to death and I have begun to clean up the shop. One of my nail technicians asks me to take a seat and allow her to do my nails. Not having them done for about two weeks, I decide to take her offer.

Just getting out of the chair, my cell phone is blowing up. I check my hands making sure that they are dry before I answer. I look at the phone and notice that the caller is Rashad. I am surprised to see him calling me so soon. I knew he was coming back today but he normally likes to make his runs before coming home.

"Baby I am about to come and get you."

"For what, Rashad?"

"I need you to follow me to drop off the rental."

"You want me to drive the rental? Where is Malik's ass?" I question with an attitude.

"No, I don't want you to drive the rental. I still have my things inside. Malik is getting dropped off at our house when I put everything up, then we will drop the rental off."

"Aw, okay. Should I close the shop for the day? Business has been slow today."
"No, don't do that. Any money is better than

none. Have one of the girls close up for tonight. I'm getting off at the exit now so I will be pulling up in a second."

"Okay I will see you." I say ending the call. Although Rashad has only been gone for the weekend I miss him dearly like every other time he leaves. More than that, Raymond misses him also, but he has begun to understand that daddy has to go on business trips.

Waiting for Rashad I'm inside the office searching on the internet for some new boots. Rashad barges in ordering for me to hurry up. I shut down my laptop and rush out the door.

When I get outside to the rental, Rashad has surprised me with gifts. Bags are everywhere in sight. I give him a hug and kiss before searching through the bags and boxes of shoes. I notice that Rashad had bought me some very expensive dresses and jeans. I pull out one pair of jeans and look at him crazy knowing my ass will be very vivid in these. He laughs at my facial expressions but I continue to search. Two of my girls come out from the shop to check out what I am pulling out. I show them a few items and then a box of heels that I know cost every bit of two thousand dollars. I am so happy that I try to put them on my feet now to show them off. Rashad begs for me to put everything back and reminds me that we have things to do. Sensing the urgency in his voice I wrap it up and tell the girls goodbye.

I rush to get into my car and follow behind them. I call Rashad, curiously asking , what was the reason behind buying me all of the gifts, but he ignores me. He puts on a front for Malik, like the money was nothing to spend on me. I go along with his front and imagine myself stepping out with Brandi in my new shit.

After clearing out the car and dropping Malik off to his busted up hood rat, I pull off without any direction. He climbs in the passenger seat taking out a knot of money. After flipping through the bills he takes out his cell phone. I wait to ask him where we are going, hearing him tell someone on the phone that we will arrive there soon. He signals for me to turn on the interstate heading towards downtown. I wonder if he has plans for us to go out to eat, doing his usual, but buying me damn near half a wardrobe is unusual. I think that maybe he is meeting with a new buyer, but why wouldn't Malik ride with him.

"I have another surprise for you." Rashad says smoothly.

"I can't wait to see."

Rashad continues to direct me without giving me a location, which has me on edge, not knowing where I am going. I am becoming irritated with him and suddenly he tells me to pull up in a parking lot. I look around for any signs of a restaurant but I do not see any nor do I smell any food.

"Come on!" he orders climbing out of the car first.

"Here I come!" I snap back applying lip gloss to my lips.

I cautiously climb out studying the area like I am some sort of investigator. I grab my purse and cell phone following right behind him. We walk rapidly towards a brick building and I notice a sign on the building telling me exactly what kind of business this is.

After being greeted at the door Rashad escorts us to a booth in the rear. I am shocked that this nigga had the audacity to bring me to a strip club. What was he thinking, I ask myself. Reframing from speaking to him I get on my phone and put a post on a social network. Rashad orders us some drinks from a waitress and asks her to bring some girls that he knew over. I look at him crazy but bite my tongue.

Minutes later, two strippers step in front of us with smiles on their faces bouncing everything that could shake. I give them a look of discuss and ask him "is he serious?"

"I thought that you would enjoy yourself here. You can do whatever you want tonight. I know how much you wanted to go down the way with me so I felt bad and thought you would like this."

"You know that I don't do this!"

"You don't now? T, cut it out." Rashad says nonchalantly.

"I'm cool."
"You can at least get a lap dance and try to have fun with your man. I have already asked them to come home with us"

"What nigga are you crazy!"

"I thought that you like keeping your man happy."

"You know that I do, but not with these bitches. I am ready to go now Rashad!" I bark standing to my feet.

The strippers quickly stop grinding on him and bouncing their asses. One of them stares me in the eye fixing her mouth to say something, but I guess she sees that I am ready to grind my heels in her ass.

I become furious and rapidly leave the club heading towards my car. I nervously fumble with keys pulling them out my purse. I look over my shoulder and see Rashad rushing in my direction. I get inside the car before he could say a word. He enters the car with an evil look on his face. I try to keep my fierce facial expression but he ignores my expression smacking me once across the face.

I am shocked grabbing my face. Warm tears dropped down my face slowly. Rashad and I have been in plenty of fights but he has never hit me, without me hitting him first.

"Don't you ever embarrass me again!" Rashad shouts from the top of his lungs.
"You must have lost your muthafucking mind putting your hands on me!" I yell.

Driving to Brandi's to pick up Raymond, we do not speak a word to the other. He is staring out the passenger window with his fist balled up on his lap. Many thoughts begin to run through my mind about his actions. I ask myself, did I really embarrass him in front of the strippers and did I play with his ego.

Pulling up to the house, soon as I put the car in park he rushes to get inside. He does not attempt to get Raymond or his backpack. I slowly walk behind him with Raymond in my arms struggling to get to the door.

When I enter the house, Rashad is not anywhere in sight. I take Raymond to his bed and decide to give Rashad some time to himself because he needs to think about what he did and said to me.

I turn the TV on and watch a recorded television series. Being distracted from what happened earlier, I am unable to give the show my full attention. I get up from my curled up position on the couch and pour myself a glass of wine. Reassuming my position, on the couch, I am distracted by the continuous chimes from Rashad's phone. Normally I do not touch his phone but it is beginning to irritate me. I quietly walk inside the bedroom and take his phone off the nightstand. I close the door behind me and take a seat at the kitchen island. I notice that he has three missed calls and has received messages. I am wondering who in the hell would be sending him a message this late at night, so I go into his message icon. The very first picture I see is a back shot picture of a girl's ass. The next message I open is a picture of a vagina. I know that the picture is not mine and more than likely it is the same girl. My blood begins to boil and I can feel my heart pound harder. I check to see who has sent the pictures and the senders name is under Devon. I know that a nigga name Devon don't have a fat ass and a pussy. As a matter of fact, Rashad does not know a Devon. Now I check the missed calls and it says Devon. I do not recognize the number, but my female instincts tell me to do some more investigation.

I check all of his recent phone calls and nothing seems out of the ordinary besides seeing that Devon calls him a lot. I go to his pictures and the first few are of our family which makes me smile and I begin to feel guilty about going through his phone. I continue to flip through wondering what other pictures he has. This sorry ass nigga has the audacity to have pictures of the strippers in his phone doing everything under the sun to each other. I begin to take rapid deep breaths seeing the next picture. Rashad has pictures of the girls sucking his dick and of him going down on each of them. I feel so sick to my stomach that I vomited inside my mouth.

I call the so called Devon and of course a females voice answers the phone. I do not waste any more time with her and rush over to the kitchen grabbing a butcher's knife.

I storm into the bedroom busting the door wide open. I throw his phone at him waking him up fully.

"Nigga, how can you cheat on me with these nasty ass hoes?"

"What in the hell are you talking about. I ain't cheating on you."

"Do I look fucking stupid to you? I saw your little ass dick on your phone with those bitches!" I snap aggressively waiving the knife in the air.

"It's not like that."

"What's it like then? Are you getting paid to be a porn star or something?" I say sarcastically.

"T, you need to calm the fuck down!" Rashad orders.

"I'm not going to calm the fuck down nigga!" I shout louder.

"If you don't get that knife out of my face I will have to beat your ass."

Ignoring his threats, I continue to waive the knife. "What are you going to do Rashad? Are you going to cry like a little bitch like when my brother..." Before I finish my sentence, Rashad has punched me once in the jaw and once in my stomach, dropping me face first to the floor. He continues to rant about my brother and how Mar doesn't want any problems with him. Rashad kicks me in my back forcing me to let out a loud cry. I ball into a fetal position and allow him to punish me some more. I lay on the floor sobbing pleading that he stop.

After what feels like hours of punishment he suddenly stops the abuse. I open my eyes believing that he has walked away and this will be my chance to get up from the floor. I see his feet in front of me then he forcefully grabs me by the hair throwing me down on the bed. Tears blur my vision but I am able to see him taking aim at me with his gun.

"Baby, please don't do this." I plead with tears racing down my face.

Rashad, looks at me and smiles. He pulls back on the hammer and signals with his free hand for me to be quiet. I let out another loud cry. I pray that God save me from this lunatic. A shadow emerges from the hallway and Raymond stagers in.

"Mommy, why are you crying?" Raymond asks walking towards me.

"Mommy is okay baby." I answer.

Raymond climbs in bed with me and I hug him tightly not knowing what Rashad has in mind. I cradle Raymond's head to my chest and rub my fingers through his curly hair, whispering to him how much I love him. My little hero, I say to myself.

Rashad lowers his gun and stares at us. I try to look him in the eye but I am too nervous that I will get a wrong reaction from him. He reaches down to grab Raymond but I pull away.

"Give him here!" Rashad orders.

"No!"

"Mommy." Raymond cries.

"Look T, you are getting the boy scared." Rashad says lowering his tone of voice.

Rashad reaches down again and Raymond lifts his arms for his father to grab him. I know that not in a million years, Rashad would not dare to hurt Raymond, but I want to make sure of that.

I wait a few seconds before trying to get Raymond, but Rashad purposely steps away from my grasp. I hop off of the bed eyeing the knife on the floor. As much as I want to dart for it I decide against it.

"Rashad give me my baby." I ask in a low tone.

"Why should I?"

"Look at him Rashad he is scared."

49

Rashad takes a brief look into Raymond's eyes and sets him down gently on the floor. Raymond rushes over to me with open arms.

"T, I want you and him to get the fuck out of my house!" He says sternly.

"What?" I ask screwing up my face not believing the words that just came out of his mouth.

"You and him, get the fuck out!" Rashad shouts pumping his fist in the air towards the door.

"You are not putting me out of my house."

"I don't want to put my hands on you but I will."

"You are a sorry ass nigga. How can you put out your wife and your son?"

"What the fuck did you just say?" Raymond asks pulling his gun out from under his shirt.

"You ain't shit Rashad. I bet you are acting like this because one of your little bitches has done put some fantasy in your head."

"I am ready to move on and the two of you are holding me back."

"That's some shit to say to your son. You are going crazy."

"I have to rush home when I am out handling

business so that you can live your high profile life. I try to make our relationship more enjoyable but you acting like you don't want to do shit anymore. T, I don't love you anymore. That is why I have been fucking both of those strippers almost every night. Shit, they can move in to take your place."

"Fuck you nigga! I knew it!" I shout at the top of my lungs.

"Yeah, yeah, yeah, just get the fuck out." He says walking behind me towards the door.

"Where am I going to go?" I ask waiting for his response.

"I don't know and I don't care. Get a hotel room or go to your mom's." Rashad replies defiantly.

"Can I at least get some of our clothes? We will then go."

"Yeah, bitch go and get your shit. You are not taking any of that new shit that I bought, anywhere. I am going to donate that to my new fund."

Taking a seat on the bed he is watching my every move. I pack a full suitcase and take all of my dresses from the closet. The only thing that is left in the closet is his stuff and a few boxes of my heels. I throw on a pair of jogging pants and running shoes. I go for the safe that is bolted down in the closet to get my jewelry and possibly take some cash but when I look over my shoulder Rashad's eyes are aimed on me.

"What the fuck you think you are about to do? Get the fuck away from my shit."

I jump back like I had gotten stung by a bumble bee. "I was going to get my shit out of the safe." I reply softly.

"Your shit? Bitch I bought all of that shit and it is staying here."

"Rashad I bought a lot of my jewelry with my own money."

"Well it ain't going anywhere. You have ten minutes to finish getting your shit, then I am throwing your ass out," he threatens holding the gun in one hand and Raymond's hand in the other.

I cannot believe that this man whom I have loved for so many years is treating me like a bitch from the streets. My eyes begin to tear up again and not wanting him to see my pain I rush over to Raymond's bedroom and quickly fill his bags.

Dragging the suitcases to the door, I take a long look around the house and memories of us fill my head. I reminisce on the day we first walked in together. We decided then that this was going to be the house that we were going to live our lives in. I think of all the family events we had here and then I think about the first time we had sex. We started in the kitchen on the island and ended up on the soft champagne colored carpet in our bedroom. Lastly I reminisce on the day we brought Raymond home from the hospital into his new home. A smile crosses my face with the thoughts, but instantly reality sets in. I am leaving those memories behind and moving on.

I toss the remaining luggage in my new BMW 3 Series which Rashad recently bought for me as a gift for our anniversary to match his BMW M5. Rashad stands in the doorway holding Raymond with a blank look on his face. I walk towards them continuing to avoid eye contact. Inches away from Rashad, Raymond jumps into my arms with laughter. I juggle with him getting him properly positioned on my waist.

"Bye daddy!" Raymond giggles.

"Rashad, when can I come back and get the rest of my things?" I ask.

"T, I don't want you anywhere near my house or my shop. I will have the locks change and your shit will go to storage. Please don't come back here trying to start any shit. I will have my new bitch in here." Rashad replies solemnly slamming the door behind him.

Safely placing Raymond in his car seat I close the door and stand perfectly still staring at the house. My body begins to tremble as tears rapidly roll down my face pouncing to the concrete driveway. Raymond knocks on the window with his toy car to get my attention. I try to regain myself and wipe away my tears but he see right through me.

"Don't cry mommy. Everything will be alright you will see." Raymond says as tears continue to cascade down uncontrollably. His words warmed my heart.

"Yes, we will son. Mommy will make sure of it, I promise."

Before getting inside the car I take a long look at my beautiful home. The yard is freshly cut and the scent from the flowers I planted fills the air. The garden lights are reflecting his car and I look around frantically for something to smash his windshield. I want him to feel some of my pain. I notice a stone near the flower bed, but I suddenly decide against something that childish. I will hurt him more than he has ever hurt me. I vowed to myself.

Exiting the driveway I press down heavily on the gas causing my tires to burn and leave a tire mark on the driveway. I look in my rearview mirror at the cloud of smoke behind me as I race up the street.

I race through the neighborhood until I reach the Morse Road I-270 ramp. I ride on the interstate confused about where I am headed. After twenty-five minutes of driving, I am near another turning point in which I could go home, back to Dayton or find a hotel nearby. Not wanting to face my mom explaining to her why I have a bruise on my face, I decide to get a hotel. I look at Raymond and he is fast asleep, so I know that my decision is right. A nice warm bed and peace of mind will help a lot.

CHAPTER 6

With Raymond fast asleep on the bed lying next to me I take some time to clear my mind. I try to fall asleep, but my mind will not allow me to get Rashad out of my thoughts. I begin to wonder how long he has been cheating on me and if his nasty ass was wearing a condom with those hoes. I think about all of the times I trusted him, to come inside me, not knowing the risk I was putting myself through. The thought alone has me hating him even more. I wonder if the strippers are the only bitches he has sex with, but I doubt that seriously. I can't help but think of him putting his nasty dick inside of these girls. I begin to feel dirty myself, imagining the things they might do on the side with other men. I cautiously slide off the bed and rush to take a shower.

Inside the shower I scrub myself clean trying to remove the filth off of my body. My mind plays the night of us inside the shower with Kyra. I feel as if I am going crazy, but I know that I need to keep it together for my little man. I stand under the shower allowing the water to flow down my body. I determine that I am going to be strong for the both of us, so I have to get him out of my mind. With little money on me and only a few thousand in my bank, I know that I have to make something happen, fast. I cannot depend on Rashad anymore. I have to do this, from this point on, not depending on any man to do anything for me. I will make sure that I will not get my emotions involved with another man, so that he can get the opportunity to hurt me.

Getting out of the shower, I wrap my hair with a towel and use another to tie over my breast. Exiting the bathroom, Raymond continues to sleep like an angel, looking just like his daddy and I cannot stand it. I take a seat on the edge of the bed and apply some lotion over my body. After pampering myself, I become bored. I flip through the channels on the television unable to find anything of interest. I turn my phone on and go to my social network to change my relationship status and post a positive comment about where my life is now. I look at my phone and notice that I have a voice mail. I wonder if Rashad felt apologetic and left a message, but when I hear the message it is from Brandi.

"Girl what's going on with you and your man? I just tried calling you to see if you wanted to step out for a few hours and Rashad answered with an attitude, snapping off at me. Rashad had the audacity to tell me not to call there anymore unless I am calling for him. He said that you don't live there and he doesn't want to see you. Can you believe that nigga girl trying to get at me? I love you T, I hope that you are handling this well. Are you done with his ass now? Turn your damn phone on girl we need to talk. Okay, just call me." Brandi said ending her message.

Brandi and I have been best friends since first grade. We attended the same schools form grade school to college. We both majored in dance but I wasn't able to finish school due to missing classes with my brother. Brandi continued and graduated getting her degree. Brandi is now a dance choreographer teaching Hip Hop dance to young girls at a dance studio. When she is not in the studio she is on somebody's dance floor entertaining whoever is watching. Brandi is a diva, buying all of the most expensive hand bags and clothing. She hustles most of her money off of men with money and sometimes even women. She don't care who is paying for her time as long as she gets paid. I respect her hustle because it is similar to mine but most of the time she don't have to show her pussy unless it benefits her more.

Brandi is very attractive and uses her beauty for both sexes. Her curvy fat ass, 36 DD breast size, chocolate skin, almond shaped eyes, and sassy attitude makes it easy to add numbers in her bank account. I love her like a sister and since we have been knowing each other, she has been there for me. We are so close that we don't have to tell the other if something is wrong, we can sense it. Tonight she must have gotten that feeling. Besides my mother, Brandi is the only person I can confide in without being judged or being put down. I know that she will listen when I call and give me the best advice, knowing me very well.

I give her a call and she does not answer on my first attempt. I call again and she answers after the second ring. When she answers I hear a lot of commotion in the background. Brandi tells me that she is in the club but decides to leave knowing that I had to talk to her.

Brandi and I talk for over an hour about Rashad. I tell her about the strip club and what I had seen in his phone. Brandi is not surprised to hear this always warning me how much of a dog Rashad is. When I tell her about the trip down to Atlanta, she screams so loud through my phone that she made Raymond turn on his side, being disturbed. She is shocked to hear that I have experienced sex with another women knowing how much I am against it when she tells me her stories. I describe what Kyra looks like from the head down, catching myself licking my lips. Knowing Brandi is waiting for the details about the sex I had with Kyra, I decide to tell her everything. I go into details of how good Kyra used her tongue to give me multiple orgasms and how good she tasted when I used my tongue. Brandi started to go crazy. I pause the conversation imagining about her again. Brandi clearly understands why I am attracted to Kyra and tries to explain the reasoning behind my feelings. I tell her that she has heard enough for the night, but urges me to tell her more. I quickly shift the conversation back on Rashad. She becomes upset and acts as if I don't want to tell her my secret. After a while she gives in knowing that I need to get the situation off my chest.

Trying to talk about what I saw in his phone, images of him fucking those girls like he had Kyra and I pop into my head. Tears fill my eyes, but Brandi being a true friend encourages me to continue. I manage to tell her how I was taunting him with the knife, but wasn't expecting him to hit me like I was a man. She cannot believe my words and I finds herself crying when I tell her that he pulled his gun on me in front of Raymond. Brandi feels my pain and goes off about not only what Rashad did to me, but the fact that Raymond had to witness his father pointing a gun at me. She begs for me to tell my brother what happened and allow him to get Rashad. I ask her to keep this between us because I know that Lamar wouldn't hesitate to kill Rashad. Rashad is my son's father so I don't want him dead but I want him to feel my pain. Brandi reminds me of everything I just said and the fact that he has played with my life in many ways. She warns me to go get a checkup from my doctor so that I can be sure if he has or has not given me any STD. I tell her that I will call the doctor but I am honestly scared to find out knowing how dirty he is. Before ending our call, Brandi asks me to stay with her until I get back on my feet. She acts as if she is doing me a favor saying how lonely she is at home by herself. Brandi assures me that I wouldn't be a burden and I am more than welcome to stay. I end the call by telling her that we will accept her invitation.

The next evening Raymond and I wait patiently out in front of Brandi's condominium. Leaving the hotel, I call her and she says that she will meet me here after work.

Brandi assures me that she will rush home to help us move our things in. I am overwhelmed by her hospitality and sincerely thankful. The only other place that I could go at this short notice was my mother's but I am not in the mood for the preaching.

Brandi swiftly pulls up alongside my car smiling from ear to ear. Raymond goes crazy in the back seat rushing me to let him out so that he can see her. Brandi spoils Raymond rotten. Every time Brandi babysits Raymond, she either takes him somewhere fun for kids or buys him whatever he picks out at the toy store. I made her his God mother, knowing that she will watch over him like her own if anything ever happened to me. Brandi climbs out of her car and quickly opens Raymond's door taking him out of the car seat. I laugh at her actions as I grab my purse and suitcase. Brandi pours on the kisses and tickles Raymond causing him to laugh uncontrollably. He squirms around in her arms trying to get away but enjoying his attention. I pop the truck showing her our belongings and she sends me a playful look like she's not going to help.

"I will get his bag and some of your dresses to help you." She says after giving me a kiss on the cheek.

Brandi puts Raymond down and he takes off towards the front door. I follow behind her as she escorts us inside the house and to my surprise she has the spare bedroom ready for me. Raymond already has his room so all we had to do is hang up the clothes I brought. Raymond sat directly in front of his 46 inch LED television to watch his movies. Brandi and I continue to unpack the car and put my things away neatly so that I will feel comfortable. As we unpack she keeps on asking me to finish telling her about Kyra and I. Brandi insists that I do not leave anything out.

She is a freak and I wouldn't think that my experience with Kyra would come close to anything she does on a regular basis but she is intrigued to know, not wanting me to miss any details.

We have our girl talk and I am done with talking about anything that I have done with Rashad. I tell her that I want to thank her by cooking a big diner.

I speed off to the nearest grocery store feeling a lot better than I did yesterday. I blast my music and sing along to the lyrics. I hurry to pick up the items I need for diner humming the last song I heard in the car. At the checkout line the cashier asks me do I want to use cash or credit. I wonder to myself if he had canceled any of the cards yet. I hesitate to pull out one of the cards but I manage to get it out. As anticipated he canceled my credit cards and to save myself from the embarrassment I pull out my bank card and pay.

Entering the house, I smile seeing Raymond and Brandi cuddled up on the couch watching an action hero movie. Raymond hears me close the door behind me and hops off the couch to help with the groceries. His actions are so amusing that I cannot resist, but laugh.

After eating our four course meal, we all feel rested. Brandi decides to wash the dishes while I give Raymond a bath and get him into bed. I sit next to him reading from a children's book and watch him slowly doze off. I creep out of his bedroom and into mine. I strip down to only my panties and bra. I prepare the water for a hot bubble bath and lite some candles so that I can relax. I slowly bathe myself enjoying some R&B music and the soft soapy wash cloth.

Back inside my bedroom, I reach down for my panties and I notice a vibrator lying on top of my pillow. I pick it up laughing knowing Brandi put it there thinking that I should use it. I walk back towards the door and close it behind me. I set myself comfortably on the pillows and allow the vibrator to put me in a sensual ecstasy.

CHAPTER 7

I wake up the next morning with the vibrator lying in-between my thighs. I laugh at the thought, placing the vibrator under the bed. I quickly get up and lay my clothes out for the day so that I can handle business. I have to call my doctor to schedule a visit, take Raymond to school, look for a place to live and try to find a job.

I finish curling my hair and rush to the kitchen to make breakfast. I make turkey and vegetable omelets, with wheat toast and sausage links. Brandi walks in looking like she is still asleep, wearing a silk leopard teddy and a scarf tied around her head.

"Damn T, you are up early this morning. I would have thought that you would still be asleep from your relaxing night." Brandi giggles before digging into her food.

"Thanks girl for introducing me to your friend, but you can have it back." I blush.

"Don't worry about it. I have more toys to please myself with."

"Girl you are a freak," I say laughing.

"Aint I," she replies staring at me.

I look back at her wondering if that was a question or a statement. I notice that her cleavage is showing and her nipples are erect.
"I am up because I have a lot to do today," I say breaking the weird moment.

Brandi smacks her lips, "T, you and Raymond have been through a lot. How about you take the day off and try to relax? Put on something comfortable, then pleasure yourself with one of my toys. I have any type of toy that will please that pussy. Stay here, I will take Raymond to school. I will also pick him up after my class is finished. This way you will and you can get that time to yourself that you desperately deserve."

"Brandi I need to get myself together before I have a nervous breakdown. So much shit is going on with me right now."

"That's why you are going to keep your ass right here and chill. We will be back later. Everything you need is in my top drawer in my nightstand. Enjoy." Brandi says walking away to her bedroom with a glass of orange juice.

I cannot help but to laugh at her, watching her walk away. Raymond shuffles his way into the kitchen with his pajamas twisted. I figured that he must have slept well because he has red marks on his face from where he laid.

"Mommy I am hungry," he says wiping his eyes.

"Boy stop it. You know that I made you something to eat. Go take a seat so that I can bring it to you."

Within minutes, Raymond has swallowed his breakfast. I feel a little bad for not believing that he was hungry. I walk up to him and give him a kiss.

"Mommy, can I go to school today?"

"Yes you can. Brandi will take you to school

today, so I want you to be good."

"I will mommy!" Raymond cheerfully shouted running off to his room.

I finished my plate and watched a few minutes of the local news before getting Raymond dressed for school. Like my little man, he had already gone into the bathroom to wash his face and brush his teeth. He is excited to go to school but after school he sometimes goes to the daycare center while I am at the shop.

Raymond sits on the couch watching cartoons and patiently waiting on Brandi. I check the time and notice that Raymond needs to be at school within thirty minutes or he will be late. Since I was always the one taking him to school and picking him up from the daycare, he has never been late. I become impatient with Brandi and storm off to her room. Brandi is sitting on the edge of her bed wearing only her panties and bra. I walk in with a lot of attitude asking if she wants me to take him, but she ignores my attitude as she applies lotion to her body. For a moment I thought that she was purposely taking her time getting dress to allow me to see her. Just as the thought came in my mind it went out. Brandi has never come at me like that and up until I told her about Kyra, she knows that I did not like women. I begin to bitch at her about how I could have taken him myself. After saying what I had to say to her she quickly gets dress and grabs her bag full of dance stuff. Opening the door to leave I ask her to take Raymond to the daycare after she picks him up from school. She don't reply with words but replies with a smirk.

"Hold up mister aren't you forgetting something?" I say acting as if I am sad.

Raymond turns around and quickly run into my arms. I give him a huge kiss and he runs to Brandi's car with laughter. I stand back up from my bent position and Brandi quickly kisses me on the lips. I am at a loss for words. Brandi has kissed me before but never on the lips. My thoughts are interrupted by a neighbor honking his horn at me. I notice that I am standing outside in a pair of boy cut shorts and a tank top revealing every curve on my body. Feeling embarrassed, I just smile and wave at the good looking man whom I believe is in his early twenty.

I shut the door behind me, flopping down on the couch laughing at the look on his face. Although I felt embarrassed at first it sure does feel good to know that I am still attractive to a fine ass man. I realize that I am single and I can please myself with whomever I want and when I want.

Suspicious thoughts cross my mind wondering what kind of toys Brandi's freaky ass could have. I know that she is a regular at the sex shops and attend many sex parties. Her collection can be outrageous with numerous things to please a woman. I leave the couch and dart to her room.

Without any hesitation I go straight for her nightstand drawer. When I open the drawer my eyes widen with shock seeing all of the different toys, flavored oils, lotions, beads, dildos, porno DVDs, and more. I grab three DVDs and sit them on the bed while I read the titles of all three. I find the erotic titles very humorous and wonder what made her choose these movies. I flip over the movies and I become shocked again, seeing actual sex scenes. The first movie has girls sucking dick and having the men have an orgasm all over their face. The second DVD catches my eye because all of the scenes are of women having threesomes with a man. I become instantly excited and my curiosity forces me to play the movie.

Only minutes into the movie I have already pulled my panties off and started to roll my finger over my clitoris. The movie is very explicit causing my pussy to become very moist. I take visual notes of the girls making each other share multiple orgasms with their tongue and various toys. I study how they use the strap-on to fuck another one and how they use the dildos. I take out a dildo and imagine Kyra using the dildo on me. I choose a nice size dildo about the same size that I was used to for years but this dick has a vibrator, for my clit. I position myself perfectly to feel every inch of the dildo but most importantly, I place the vibrator directly on my clit. The vibration is driving me insane but I cannot resist and want more. I pull back my legs and I allow the dildo to work on my G-spot so damn good that I squirt all over Brandi's comforter. I lay back on her pillows gasping for air as if I were in the porno myself.

Ring! Ring! Brandi's house phone suddenly rings in my ear. Lazily I reach over to answer.

"Hello," I say breathing heavily.

"Are you busy?" Brandi asks knowingly.

"Girl shut up," I say playfully.

"I told you that you would find something to take care of that pussy." Brandi teased jokingly.

"Girl you are so nasty. I did need this time to relax."

"Relax my ass. You were busy making yourself come." Brandi giggles.

"Yes I was." I laugh also.

"I guess I'm not the only freak. You are showing your true colors T. I will allow you to finish relaxing."

"Alright. Bye Brandi," I say ending the call.

After putting her blanket into the washing machine and cleaning off the dildo, I go directly for the shower. I hurry to clean myself so that I can still handle some business.

I do not hesitate to call my doctor and schedule a visit for today. I have a few hours before my appointment so I search the internet for jobs that I find of interest. I apply for jobs that are clerical and some retail positions. The retail jobs that I apply for are stores that I shop at on a regular basis. I hope that I am able to get an interview with any of them and hopefully a job. I would love to receive discounts from my favorite stores. I end my job search after applying for four clerical jobs and three retail stores.

"Treasure!" The nurse shouts, calling me to come to the back.

I quickly undress as asked by the nurse. I sit patiently waiting in the examination room for my doctor to come in. I begin to worry if I have a STD and if I do should I tell Rashad.

The doctor enters the room with a concerned look on his face. He asks what has brought me in today as if

67

he did not know. I told the nurse everything and now he wants to hear the embarrassing details for himself? I start off the conversation by telling him that I do not have any symptoms of any STDs but I am concerned because Rashad has had multiple partners. The doctor immediately asks me to lye back so that he can check my vagina. I allow him to check me for every STD. I had to take the urine test before I was shown my room for examination. The doctor leaves the room to check my tests and brings back my results. All of these tests have me furious at Rashad for putting me through all of this. I sit for a few minutes allowing myself to get my thoughts together for whatever the doctor has to say. I get up from the table and get fully dress before the doctor gently knocks on the door to enter. I study his facial expressions carefully before he has a chance to say a word. The doctor takes a seat right in front of me, removing his eye glasses from his face. I brace myself against the table waiting for the results. I am becoming nervous and anxiety builds in my chest with the thought of the doctor telling me that I am pregnant or that I have a STD. He looks me in the eye and tells me that I need to have safe sex and no sex is the safest sex, like this is some new shit for me. I interrupt his schooling and ask him bluntly "What are the results?" He tells me that I am negative for all STDs and that I am not pregnant. I am so relieved. The doctor does give me a prescription, for depression and asks that I take it easy for a few days. I tell him that I am moving forward and I am not looking back.

I leave the doctor's office heading for Raymond's daycare center. Although I am negative with all of my results, I continue to think of how Rashad can have sex with these hoes knowing he could be giving me something. I wonder, when was the last time that he was truly in love with me. I honestly believe that he has falling out of love with me and not knowing why is killing me.

I am near Raymond's daycare center and I am eager to get back to Brandi's house to relax. I call the daycare to let them know that I will be arriving soon but they tell me that Brandi has already come and picked Raymond up. I do not show any attitude and politely end the call. Soon as I end the call with the daycare I dial Brandi.

"What up T?" Brandi questions.

"Tell me why I drove over to the daycare and found out that Raymond wasn't there?"

"He is with me. You remember that I told you that I was going to pick him up after my last class?"

"No I don't. I'm sure that you probably did. Girl my head has been spinning a hundred miles an hour. I am not myself right now."

"I understand." Brandi says sympathetically.

"I'm going to get it together. I am still fucked up over everything."

"You don't have to tell me. That is why I am going to make sure that you will be able to relax and get everything off of your mind."

"You don't have to do anything for me girl."

"Yes I do, you are my girl." Brandi says ending the call.

When I pull up to Brandi's condo, Brandi and Raymond are standing on the porch to greet me. I feel a lot better seeing people that genuinely love me. Raymond patiently waits for me at the entrance chewing on a piece of candy. I kneel down getting eye level with him and give him a big hug Raymond kisses me on the cheek leaving his slobber on me.

"I ordered some pizza and I have a movie on for him but we can watch something else latter," Brandi announces.

"Thanks. That will be fine. Where is the food? I have not eaten since this morning."

"Take a seat I will bring you some slices ," she orders.

I sit next to Raymond enjoying the hot pizza and his laughter. Raymond is in another world enjoying this movie and his happiness is priceless.

Raymond falls asleep mid-way through the movie. Brandi gets up from her comfortable position on the loveseat and carries him to his bedroom. I sprawl out on the couch trying to find something for us to watch. Brandi re-enters the room and lifts my head off the pillow to place it in her lap. I take this time to thank her for everything and tell her about my day. Brandi acts surprise hearing me talk about putting in applications. We laugh at the idea of me working for someone else other than myself. She tells me that I don't have to be in a rush to get a job and just take this time to get myself together emotionally. Brandi promises me that she will help me get over Rashad. She helps me remember the days when I was independent doing everything on my own long before I met Rashad. Brandi asks about the results and I proudly tell her that I am clean but the doctor did prescribe depression medicine. Brandi and I continue to talk as we drink a bottle of wine. Already having drunk two glasses I remind myself to take my pills. I try getting up but Brandi playfully holds me down stressing to me that she's doing everything for me tonight. She rushes to bring back my pills and I swallow the pills down with another glass of wine. We finish talking about my day and decide on a movie.

Watching the movie I can feel the medicine and alcohol taking effect. I leave the couch without giving her an explanation. Brandi hops off the couch turning the television off and begins to follow behind me. She asks again why I am leaving her alone on the couch and I tell her that the medicine has me feeling sleepy. I don't go directly for my bedroom but I turn on the shower so that it will be hot when I step in. Her facial expression shows that she is disappointed at me for not hanging in there. I ignore her ass and strip all of my clothes off. I notice that Brandi is staring directly at me as she sips on her wine. I walk pass her brushing my breast on hers as I rush to the bathroom closing the door behind me.

Stepping out of the shower I slip on the floor but quickly regain my balance before falling. I brace myself against the sink counter as I try to tie the towel around my body. I open the door slowly and walk to my room watching each step. When I enter the room I quickly take a seat on the bed. I begin to feel my eyes becoming heavy so I try to lotion my body as fast as I can. I give up on trying to lotion the lower half of my body and fall back on the pillows closing my eyes tightly.

I fall asleep dreaming about Rashad and I making

love on our honeymoon in Barbados. He kisses and licks every inch of my body perfectly. His touch is soft and sensual. Rashad flips me over on my stomach and slides gently inside of me penetrating deeply. I reach down to feel my wetness before licking my juice off my fingers. The dream is all too real because I can feel his breath on my neck. I feel a soft kiss on my neck and without opening my eyes I turn my body over and I receive another kiss on the lips. This kiss is passionate and the touch is soft. I don't hesitate to exchange kisses tasting the watermelon flavor from this stranger's lips. The lips from of the stranger travels along my neck to my breast. I crack my eyes open and to my surprise this stranger who is scrolling their tongue down my stomach is Brandi. I close my eyes tight anticipating for her to taste my nectar. I spread open my legs further apart for easier access. She takes my invitation and swiftly swirls her tongue over my clit. Brandi uses her tongue perfectly in a sweeping circular motion. I encourage her to continue and she sticks two of her fingers inside my wet pussy causing me to let out a sensual moan. Using the tips of her fingers she applies pressure against my vaginal wall. Sexual tension builds inside me causing me to crawl all over the bed. I reach down to grab her head but she throws my hands aside. I clinch tightly on a pillow letting out all of my emotions. My body begins to tremble as she continues to flick her tongue over my clit while simultaneously thrusting her fingers. I move the pillow away from my face and I relax allowing myself to have an orgasm. Brandi laughs at the sounds I am making and becoming embarrassed I again cover my face with a pillow.

"You enjoyed that didn't you? You don't have to be ashamed of having an orgasm with me Treasure." Brandi says trying to pull the pillow away from me.

I fight to keep the pillow on my face until Brandi gives up. I feel the weight on the bed shift as she gets up from the bed. I remove the pillow away from my face and Brandi is taking off her lace thong panties at the foot of the bed. I honestly do study her body but I am studying how to move my body seductively like a professional dancer.

"I'll be right back," she says purposely walking out the room swaying her hips for me to see her ass.

Remaining in the same position since Brandi left I close my eyes and think about what just happened. I wonder what made her want to have sex with me. If I would have known how good Brandi was at oral sex I probably would have been bi-sexual years ago. I imagine how my life could be in a relationship with a women. If I were to choose to be with a woman I would have to be with Kyra. Something besides sex has me stuck on her. Just thinking about Kyra is arousing me again. I slide my hands down till I feel my wetness. A light touch causes me to tense up from the sensitivity. My clit feels swollen. I cannot imagine my clit going through another round of pleasure again.

Brandi slowly creeps back into the room closing the door behind her. I notice that she has a handful of sex toys and an oil bottle. She places the items down before turning off the lamp and turns on the television for some light. Brandi picks up a long black dildo and licks it like it is a man. She lyes on the opposite end of the bed, so that I can have a front row seat for a show. After lubricating it, she takes the dildo inside of her moist pussy. I hear her pussy lips smack as she slides the dildo inside. I watch her facial expression to see how she enjoys herself. Brandi starts to moan and thrust the dido faster. While watching her I begin to caress my breast and feel on my body wishing that

73

someone was touching me. Brandi catches me touching myself so she takes my hand and place it on the dildo signaling for me to assist her. I use the dildo like I used the one under the bed on myself. Brandi has an orgasm in no time. I take the dildo out of her and sit it in-between us. Brandi doesn't take this time to relax and enjoy her orgasm but instead rush to please me. She sits up and places a soft kiss on my breasts. After teasing me with kisses, she takes each of my nipples into her mouth sucking them to my delight. Brandi skillfully uses her hands to caress my breast and my thighs. I grab her hand that is caressing my breast and signal for her to take the dildo inside me. I lay back and allow her to please me. She skillfully maneuvers the dildo in and out of my pussy. Brandi asks me to sit up so that she can place a pillow under my back and I curiously comply. The pillow adds an extra sensual pleasure having the dido perfectly hit my G-spot. The dildo is at work but Brandi scrolls her tongue over my clit sending me into ecstasy. I cannot take all of this so I snatch the dildo away from her and toss it to the floor. Brandi steps up her tongue game and rapidly plays with my clit. I feel her hit my spot so I forcefully grab her head and keep her tongue directly on it. Brandi likes my aggressiveness and aggressively sucks my clit. I let go of her head and let out a scream squirting my juices into her mouth. My orgasm doesn't stop Brandi from eating my pussy, but adds fuel to the fire. She covers my mouth and asks me to close my eyes. I agree to her request closing my eyes. Brandi stands up and continues to tell me to keep from looking. I smile with anticipation feeling her hands glide down my thighs. With her fingers she applies some warming oil on my sensitive clit. I take two of my fingers forming the letter "V" with my pussy lips giving Brandi a perfect visual to see how wet I remain. Brandi dives in once again. After a few teasing licks on my clit she stop. I beg her to continue but she tells me that she has something better. She gently turns me over on my stomach and then positions me in doggy-style.

"Shake that ass for me!" Brandi orders slapping me hard on the ass.

Being slapped on the ass feels all too familiar. Rashad use to hit my ass for his amusement liking the way I throw my ass back when he does it. I roll my ass for her as she continues to slap my ass. She switches from slapping my ass to caressing every curve on my body. Brandi reaches between my thighs and rubs her fingers through my lips making sure that I am wet. She spreads my ass cheeks apart sticking a strap-on dick inside me. I breathe in heavily enduring the thickness of the dick. I gasp taking in the pain tightly gripping onto the covers. Brandi strokes me like a man and I am loving all of it. My once muffled moans become screams of agony. I would not have ever thought that a rubber dick would feel so good to fuck. My pussy is throbbing so bad, but I continue to keep up with her rhythm. I can't help but to tense up when Brandi tries to pound me harder and she notices the pain I am in pulling out. I think that we are done but Brandi begins to swirl her tongue inside my pussy. I fall on my stomach and quickly try to close my legs but Brandi flips me over trying to straddle me. I look at her crazy and forcefully push her away. Since I have been here at Brandi's, I have found out more about myself sexually that I would not have experienced at home.

"Alright girl shit we are done!" I shout playfully.

"Done! We are just getting started. We have all night."

"Shit no we don't." I say with a confused look.

"Yes we do. I can call off tomorrow and let the older girls teach my classes."

"You have it all planned out."

Brandi climbs off the bed taking off the strap-on. "It's your turn T." Brandi smiles.

"My turn to do what?" I ask knowingly seeing her holding the strap-on out for me to grab.

"Your turn to put it on."

"I can't do it." I say shaking my head with nervousness.

"Yes you can. Just put it on and do to me what you think I would like or better yet, do what makes you feel good."

"I'm saying that I can't because I can't. "

"What do you mean? You didn't say that when I was fucking you a second ago!" Brandi snaps.

"Brandi that shit just happened! You are my girl. Shit you are my son's God mother."

"Okay and …"

"This isn't right."

"I don't see why not. We have been friends forever and we can now be together. I just showed you what I could offer you on a daily basis."

"Brandi I just don't see you like that. We are friends and that is where I want to keep it. Besides I am still married and who knows."

"What! T, you are acting like a silly dumb ass bitch! I cannot believe that you are still on that nigga. That is what this is over. The nigga is a dog and has showed you. Not to mention he has tried to get in my panties a million times."

"Yeah, the fuck right. That nigga is what he is, but he wouldn't dare talk to you." I aggressively respond.

"Well he has. I never wanted to tell you but when you were acting stingy when you were pregnant with the pussy he use to beg me to let him taste mine."

"Bitch you are lying." I say waving her off.

"What do I have to lie for? I didn't want to tell you because I didn't want to risk ending y'all's marriage."

"That's some bullshit bitch. You are supposed to be my best friend."

"I know." Brandi says in a low tone.

"Did you fuck him?"

"Only, once. He kept begging me asking me over and over. The only reason why we did it was because he made me an offer that I couldn't refuse."

"What did he offer you? Some money?"

"Why you are trying to play me, yes he did offer me some money but that was just to eat my pussy."

"You are a hoe."

"You can say whatever, but your man offered you to me if I had sex with him. He played you like the hoe mommy." Brandi says rolling her neck.

Tears begin to fall down my face. I've never felt so betrayed and embarrassed by people who claim that they love me.

"Get the fuck out of my face Brandi. I hate your trifling ass and I will be getting the fuck out of here soon. We are no longer friends and I think that it will be best if you stay the fuck away from me."

"Whatever, bitch." Brandi says leaving the room.

CHAPTER 8

So here it is, three days later. Three days after Brandi and I had sex and had that argument. We have not said a word to each other unless we had to speak for Raymond's benefit.

Pulling up to her condo after a pointless interview I notice that she is home early. I wonder, what is her excuse for leaving the studio early this time. I open the door and music is blasting from the stereo. I search the room for the remote to turn the sound down but Brandi enters the living room looking at me like she doesn't recognize me.

"You get a job?" she questions finally speaking to me first.

"No. That was the second job that has denied me. I don't know what to do. I only have so much saved up and I still need to get me and little man a place." I reply with a frail tone.

"Girl you don't have to rush to get out of here. Besides I know how you can get some money."

"I'm not calling Rashad or my brother."

"I wasn't about to say that. Just come with me to this party. I have to meet some of my friends but I will make sure that you are cool to get in." Brandi says writing down the address to the party.

I pick up the piece of paper noticing that this party is in a rich suburb of Columbus. I turn to ask Brandi about this party but she has already left the house. I wonder what kind of party this could be, but if I am to go I want to be dressed nice.

Inside the bedroom I pull out a pair of dresses, but I didn't feel confident that I should wear something so formal. Knowing that if Brandi, is going to a party for money, then I had to wear something more sexy, but also classy. I decide to wear a silk jersey dress that hugs my body tight to show off all of my curves. I add a pair of sequined leather sandals and big gold earrings to match my shoes.

I put the address into my navigational system and follow the directions until I pull up to a multimillion dollar home. This house made my house look like an abandoned home in the worst part of any major city. I notice Brandi's car parked next to a gang of muscle cars and luxury cars. I pull in front of the house and a valet driver takes my car and parks it. I wonder who in the hell Brandi had to fuck to be invited here. I carefully walk up the stone steps hearing laughter from the security men at the door.

"Why are y'all laughing at me?" I ask staring at the sexy buff men.

"It's just all of the ladies are walking up like you." One of the men spoke.

After showing my ID the men allow me in. I take notice of the vaulted ceilings and amazing art work. I am more interested in finding out who owns this house so that I can complement them on their taste in art. I always wanted a house laid out from the inside out. I continue to pace through the house until I find a group of people in what seems to be the party room. Unable to recognize any familiar faces I take a seat at a bar which is long enough to be in a club. I order a drink and turn to watch everyone mingle. I notice models walking around with a record label print on their T-shirts. They are constantly being asked to take pictures with random men. I finally recognize a group of men that are in the music business that rap here locally. These men don't only rap they sell their share of drugs also. All of the men in the room begin to holler and move closer towards Brandi and her friends. Everyone from the bar including women leave to watch the show. I wave at Brandi when she looks my way and ask the bartender to make me another drink. I sip on my drink watching Brandi slow wine to the music. Brandi has these men mesmerized by the way she moves her body like a Jamaican dance hall queen. Suddenly a big and tall brother takes a seat next to me. I look at him telling him with my eyes that there are other seats available.

"How are you doing?" the man ask confidently.

"I'm doing just fine." I say looking at the big dark skinned brother. He is dressed nicely and his dreads are tied back showing off his razor hair line and diamond ear rings. I'm not into big brothers but for his size he is very handsome.

"Why are you sitting all alone?"

"I'm not." I say quickly to show off my wedding ring that I have yet to take off.

"Where is he? He shouldn't leave you sitting here all alone. I know I wouldn't."

"He decided to stay home. I'm here with my

81

girl."

"Who's your girl? I know everyone here." He questions looking around the room.

"You sure do ask a lot of damn questions. Matter of fact who are you?" I question with an attitude.

"My name is Bricks but you can call me Brian," he answers putting out his hand, introducing himself.

"Bricks?" I ask laughing.

"Yeah, that's what they call me."

"Can I ask why?"

"That's a lot of questions," he says playfully laughing.

"Okay, now you are a comedian." I can't help but to laugh from his humor.

Brian and I continue to talk and share jokes with one another. I notice the diamonds on his wrist and both pinky fingers. I quickly add up the estimation for his bracelet and rings. Interested to find out more about him and what he does, I ask. Brian tells me that he is a music producer from Miami but has lived up here for three years finding talent and making beats. My old instincts arise and I begin to wonder how much money this man has. I ask him multiple questions about the business to see how deep his pockets are. He assures me that the business is not all that I assume it to be. I ask him about the guys whom I recognize and he tells me that they are great rappers but they don't give their music one hundred percent of their dedication. Lastly I ask about this beautiful home that we are in. Brian tells me that he bought the house when he first came here. I look at him with disbelief thinking that he is talking shit. I know that this house is worth at least five million dollars. Brian doesn't try to convince and leaves the conversation where it is. Someone walks up on him and whispers in his ear receiving his full attention. I turn away from him acting as if I am not interested in him anymore but I am listening to every word.

"I apologize, but I have to entertain my guess. If you decide to leave before I am able to talk to you again please call me." Brian says handing me a business card walking away.

I take his card and read it before I put it in my purse. The dancers stop dancing after Brian takes the microphone and thanks everyone for coming to his birthday party. He makes another joke asking everyone not to fuck up his shit while they are here. I laugh, knowing that he is being funny towards me. Brandi suddenly runs up on me hugging all of the air from my lungs. She leans in for a kiss but I lean away.

"I see you girl." Brandi says with excitement.

"You see what?"

"I see you trying to get you a man. I ain't mad at you," Brandi says playfully pushing me.

"Aw, Brian. He is a nice guy"

"Damn he told you his government name. He must like you. T, you need to give him some of that pussy.

When I say that the man has money, he has money."

"I'm not a gold digger."

"Bitch, you know how many girls would love the opportunity to fuck him. Shit I will fuck his fat ass for a stack of money."

"You are such a hoe," I giggle with the thought of her fucking any man with money.

"I am but I have already made two thousand dollars tonight. You need to use that body of yours to get paid like me."

"Two thousand?"

"Yup. You see all I have to do. Put on a little show for these thirsty ass clowns and the money falls. We have another show tomorrow if you want to make some money or you can keep wasting time applying for jobs that are not going to hire you."
"I'm on it."

After talking to Brandi I left the party. My stomach was growling uncontrollably and although there was food at the party, I didn't want to eat in front of strangers. I decided to stop at a twenty four hour diner and pig out.

Being at home alone is boring. I check my email to see if any jobs have decided to get in contact with me but my inbox did not have a single job. I pull out Brian's business card and contemplate if I should call. I play with the card until I build up enough courage to call.

Brian and I talk on the phone for hours. I tell him about Rashad and how I am currently struggling to find a job. Brian is real understanding and does more listening than speaking. I feel like he and I have a lot in common and I feel a sense of comfort when I talk to him. Ending our call, I notice that we spent over two hours on the phone and I cannot wait to go on our upcoming date.

CHAPTER 9

Coming back from my nice evening dinner with Brian I stand on the porch waving as he leaves. The night was remarkable. Brian picked me up in his new foreign sports car and greeted me with flowers. I did not want him to meet Raymond so soon but he insisted on meeting him. Raymond acted a little angry knowing that I was going out with this strange man but his attitude quickly changed after Brian had a toy super hero for him. From the time I opened the door till the time I closed the door behind me, Brian was a perfect gentleman. I know that all relationships start off this way but I believe that he is genuinely a good person.

Brian has to go back home for a week but he wants to hook up soon as he can, but I tell him that I would like to take the relationship slow. He did not understand my reasoning and I does not try to explain. I am putting my guard up not allowing him to get too close, too fast. I want us to take our time to get to know each other and I want to make sure that this nice guy is what I get long term.

Walking in the house Brandi is rushing me to get dress. I almost forgot that we were dancing for a bachelor's party tonight. Brandi tosses me some lingerie to wear for the night. I look at the items in disbelief. She gives me some clothes that have "hoe" written all over it. I don't mind wearing a teddy and some heels but a corset with panties that has the crotch out is not happening. I throw the clothes on the floor and dig in her closet for something more of my liking. Brandi has so many lingerie outfits that she has yet to wear. I pick a see through teddy with some thong panties to show off my ass. I have the perfect pair of heels to match the lavender teddy. I hurry to put everything in a duffle bag including some baby oil to have my body glistening.

We arrive at the hotel before the other girls so I am nervous as hell. Brandi knocks on the hotel suite door and a young man opens the door smiling from ear to ear showing off diamonds in his mouth. I am instantly turned off and ready to go, but Brandi pulls me in. We dart for a spare room to change. Two other girls show up which gives me confidence to get this money because although they are cute they don't have much of a body. One of the girls, who is of Asian descent, has multiple tattoos on her body, but what freaks me out is her piercings. She has piercings on her nipples, belly button, inside of her dimples, and what I think is painfully crazy she has one in her clit.

Brandi peeks out the door and tells us that there are a lot of men out there. I hear a lot of them talking about us waiting to be entertained. The music starts to blast through the speakers signaling that it is party time.

"Are you ready for these tricks to put some money in your pocket?" Brandi asks trying to motivate me.

"Yeah girl I'm ready." I reply.

We step out into the room and all eyes are on us. The men begin to holler and throw money in the air. The three of them attack the crowd and go to work. I slowly find the courage to find the ugliest guy in the room and give him a lap dance. I slow grind on his dick until I feel his man hood harden. I stand up teasing him with touching myself and grabbing on my breast. He takes out a fist full of money and politely hands it over. I stuff the money in my bra and give him another lap dance for his gratitude. Walking towards the girls some nigga slaps my ass and throws a few bills at me.

My intention is to slap his ass but I play him by slowly bending over to pick up the money just for him to see my thong. I pick up the four bills and throw them back at him. I walk away with an attitude, but I aggressively make the spot light shaking my ass and allowing the men to get a visual of my pussy print. Brandi tag teams with me giving the men a show. She gets behind me and caresses my body. I act as if her touch is driving me crazy. The men ignore the other girls and are tossing money at us begging for us to take it to another level. Brandi decides to get totally naked and spread apart her chocolate thick thighs showing the crowd her pink passion. I am shocked by her going all the way out like this. I try to get some of her shine so I begin to twirk my ass rapidly. The men shout at the top of their lungs amazed how I am working my ass to the beat. I turn around to look at their face but I look into the eyes of someone that I instantly recognize.

Standing behind the crowd is Malik. He is staring at me weirdly and I am wondering what is going through his mind. I just hope that he doesn't tell Rashad what he is seeing. The Asian girl tries to grind on him but he is not paying her any attention. I continue to dance for the men trying to get every dollar from their pockets.

When our show ends, Brandi and I both have made over three thousand dollars which was my goal for the night. The other girls also made some money but I noticed that they had an attitude towards me. I guess I was taking their money that they would have made if I wasn't there.

With Brandi driving, I am in deep contemplation about Malik witnessing me dancing. I feel a sense of guilt and my stomach begins to ache.

"What's on your mind Treasure?" Brandi wonders trying to look me in the eye but I avoid eye contact.

"I saw Malik at the party tonight." I answer.

"Okay. What's the problem?"

"I don't want him running his damn mouth to Rashad and then I have to deal with his bullshit." I say with a lot of attitude slapping my hands together.

"Why are you worried about Rashad? Trust me he is not worried about you. He probably has one of his girls over there now."

"You are probably right."

"I know that I am. He is a big hoe," she replies solemnly.

"Do you feel bad doing this?" I ask in a low tone of voice.

"Doing what, dancing. Hell no! Those niggas are not worried about blowing money when all they do is hustle in the streets. They are paying for a fantasy and if they want a taste of the pussy then I will get them to pay again."

"I feel dirty. I don't think I will be able to do this again."

"That's okay girl but what are you going to do to keep money in your pockets. Don't think that Rashad is going to put money in your pockets for nothing. You're either going to have to give him some or somebody else for them to come out of the pockets."

"I have some money put aside to keep myself above water for now. I will have to call my brother because I can't be doing this."

"Well do what you have to do. I will support you either way. Like I said before, you are more than welcome to stay for however long."

"Thanks girl but you need your space. I have found an apartment that's in my price range until I get with my brother. I know he has some niggas lined up for me to set up."

"Just be careful, T."

"I will."

CHAPTER 10

Raymond and I have been living in our apartment for three weeks now and he has yet to adjust to his new surroundings. I try taking him outside to our apartment complex's park to meet friends but he insists on staying in the house to play with his toys. It hurts knowing my son was truly happy at home with all he could ask for.

I have not spoken with Brandi since I have left her place but I know that Raymond would love to see her. I call and ask her if he could spend the night at her house while I am out handling business. Brandi says that she has a date, but she will cancel it to be with Raymond. I thank her and quickly take him to her.

Climbing back in the car after dropping Raymond off, I don't hesitate to call Lamar about this set up that he has for me. I do not have a choice but to ask my brother for his help to get me back on my feet. Lamar does not ask why after so long I'm willing to do dirt again, but figures that Rashad isn't giving me any money for myself.

Lamar has me robbing a young boy that is coming up fast in the dope game with his boys. Lamar tells me a little information about him so I have to do my own research. I manage to meet him on my own at a night club. He is very interested in me because I act as if I am not into him and that must have done the trick knowing how these young girls throw themselves at hustlers.

The young dealer allows me to ride around with him showing me where he sells his product thinking that I am attracted to his hustle. He is just giving me easy access to rob his ass without all of the dramatics of kidnapping him.

After picking up some money from one of his dope spots he hands me one thousand dollars. I accept the money and ask him to take me shopping. He tells me that we can go shopping but after that he wants to show me his place. This stupid boy wants to keep giving me opportunities to get him for more. More than likely he has a stash at his house like many others I have robbed before. I stare at his handsome young face and decide against allowing my brother and his goons to get close to him. Knowing how Lamar is, this face will be fractured or scared up badly for Lamar's amusement.

Inside the dressing room in the department store, I give Lamar the addresses to the spots that I knew had drugs or money inside them. Lamar thought that I had lost my touch because it took me a while to get close to the boy, but he is confident that we will get paid off this job.

I must have stopped in every store that I like buying anything that I wanted with his money. I allow him to see me in a lingerie outfit just to keep him, to dig in his pockets. I am amused knowing that he won't ever see me in any of these clothes. His phone begins to ring constantly and with each ring he is shouting in the phone allowing other customers to hear his conversation. I act as if I am concerned, but I am laughing on the inside.

Lamar and his boys hit two spots taking everything they saw within a matter of minutes. By his attitude I can tell that Lamar and I will be counting a lot of bills tonight.

"I'm sorry but I have to handle something. Can

you catch a cab to your house because I have to handle some business," he says frenzied.

"Yes I'm cool." I say giving him a light hug.

"I will call you later."

No you won't I say to myself. I bought this minute phone just for your ass. I throw the phone out the window as I pull away in the cab.

I have the cab driver take me to my car which is parked in another apartment complex parking lot. I tip the driver one hundred dollars for putting my bags in my trunk.

I call Brandi to check on Raymond and she tells me that she is at Rashad's with him. I go off on her wondering why she would disrespect me by taking him over there. Brandi claims that Raymond wanted to see his dad. I tell her to meet me at her house so that I can get my son. Brandi acts as if she doesn't understand my frustration, but complies with my demand.

I speed to her house getting there in record time. I am furious with her actions. Luckily she is not here yet because I don't know what I would have done to her. She pulls up thirty minutes after my arrival climbing out trying to explain again, but I ignore her ass putting Raymond in his car seat.

"Brandi I'm not trying to hear any of that shit. I don't want my son around that sorry ass nigga and now I'm thinking that I don't want him around you because you know how I feel about him."

"That's his dad T."

"I'm his dad bitch!" I shout having my voice echo in the parking lot.

"Whatever." she says with an attitude.

"Mommy stop fighting!" Raymond cries.

"Mommy is alright baby. Brandi since you want to disrespect me and my son please don't come around me anymore."

"What?" she questions screwing up her face.

I don't waste any more time explaining to her why she is wrong. I slam my door and speed off just as fast as I pulled up.

CHAPTER 11

Ring. Ring. My doorbell chimes interrupting me from getting dress. I rush to open the door and the delivery man has two dozen long stem roses for me. I invite him in to place the roses down on my dining table. I attempt to tip the man but he rejects my offer saying that he has already been tipped generously.

Closing the door behind the delivery man, I open the card that is lying next to the flowers. The card is from Brian saying that he just wanted to put a smile on my face today. This man has ways to make me happy but after my horrible relationship with Rashad, I am unable to truly trust a man with my heart.

Brian calls me every day wanting to do something with me but I pick and choose when I want to be with him. I don't want him to feel like I am using him for his kindness or time so I try to keep my distance. Although I am very into him and would like to get to know him better, I am not ready for that relationship mentally, knowing what he wants from me. Brian is ready for a wife, a family, and someone to share is life with but I'm not ready.

Lately, I have been talking to Kyra and she wants to move here with me. We have become real close and I have been able to talk to her about anything like I used to with Brandi. Kyra was having trouble with her job so I told her about what I do for a living. She is shocked to hear that I rob men when she believes that all women that do my kind of work are hood rats.

On my way to Port Columbus to pick Kyra up from the airport, Brian calls to see if I can come over his house for dinner. This man says that he will cook me dinner and after dinner give me a massage. I think to myself that I would enjoy a good relaxing massage but I have Kyra all to myself tonight.

"I would love to come over, but I my girl is coming here from out of town."

"That's all right. We will hook up again some other time. Give me a call," he says sadly.

"I will do that."

I notice Kyra talking to some man dressed up in a business suit. I believe that he is trying to get some ass from her so when I pull up I call for her like I am her man. Kyra smiles and waves at me walking toward the car. I help her with her bags and give her a passionate kiss in front of the man. He laughs at my actions before he hops in a taxi cab.

I rush to get back to my apartment because I have planned for Kyra and I to have a wild night. When we enter the house I show Kyra the apartment leaving my bedroom for last. She knows what's on my mind so she quickly rushes me to get undress.

"Where is your son?" she asks looking behind her towards the door.

"He is staying with my mom for the night so we have the place to ourselves."

I take her to the bed making sure that I keep full control. I use some of the tricks she used on me as well as some toys that I learned about, being with Brandi. Kyra loves how I am stroking her with the strap on and slapping her ass when she bounces back. After I introduce the perfect clit vibrating dildo to her, she is done for the night.

I get up early the next morning and prepare my food for a barbeque that I have planned for her. I want to introduce her to my brother and his friends since she is joining the business.

I look outside my bedroom window and hear Lamar's music blasting in my parking lot. I become furious knowing that I have some nosey old neighbors that will be quick to tell management, or worse call the police. Before Lamar and Scotty have a chance to come in the door, I am ranting about his music. I take this opportunity to tell them that one of them has to put the meat on the grill. Scotty reluctantly says that he will do it. I escort him to the kitchen and give him the meat to cook.

A few girls from the nail shop that I have a good relationship with come by along with Lamar's friends. We are having a nice time playing cards, dominoes, and sharing conversation. The girls from the shop try to get with Lamar, but he acts as if he has a women already.

"T can you get me some more of these baked beans?" A girl asks.

"Yeah, no problem."

I rush into the house to get her food like a good hostess but while I am scooping the beans onto the plate, I hear some strange noise coming from the back. I place the plate down and walk slowly towards the noise. The closer I get towards my bedroom the more I recognize the noise. I gently push open the door and all I can see is Kyra's breast bouncing up and down. Lamar is laid back enjoying the ride of his life. With her eyes closed tightly she is unable to see my fist hitting her in the face. She falls off of Lamar's dick and onto the bed. I pick her up by her hair and continue to do damage to her face until my brother pulls me off.

"Get off of me Lamar!" I shout looking at her bloody face with disbelief.

"T you are going to kill her!" He shouts forcefully pulling me off of Kyra.

"Let go of me nigga!" I say balling my fist up again.

"Treasure I am sorry." Kyra cries.

"Fuck you bitch you need to get your shit out of my house!"

"T…" Lamar tries to speak.

"Lamar don't say shit to me. I don't believe you played me over some pussy." I say walking away.

I sit in the front room patiently waiting for Kyra and Lamar to get out. The girls did not say a word to me and just left knowing how pissed I can get. Lamar's friends are talking shit to him playfully, but I don't find anything humorous.

Lamar now fully dressed walks out with Kyra and her suitcases. Kyra quickly walks out the door without looking in my direction or speaking. I slam the door behind them and slide to the floor weeping like a baby.

I begin to believe that I cannot trust anybody but myself. I allowed Kyra to have a piece of my heart for her to shatter it. I really thought that Kyra would have completed me and I would've been able to start my life over with her.

I lye on the floor crying until I cannot cry anymore. I had to talk to somebody before I lose my mind. Brandi is out of the question after she told me what she did with Rashad. I want to talk to somebody who will listen, so I call Brian.

CHAPTER 12

I have not done a job with Lamar since the youngster and my pockets are not happy. My rent is due tomorrow and I don't have enough money to pay the rent, utilities, gas for the car, or Raymond's child care. I decide that I have to call Rashad and stop trying to take care of everything on my own. I have not asked for a penny from him so giving me some money shouldn't affect anything that he is doing.

"Rashad I need some help with your son."

"Is that right? Now you need me. I hear that you are living good over there."

"I need some money to pay his day care and a few other bills."

"I can give you the money for his day care but I'm not paying for your bills that your man can pay for."

"Stupid, I don't have a man. If I don't have the money by tonight, I will lose this apartment. Do you want your son homeless?

"He can always come back home." Rashad chuckles.

"My son will not ever live with you! Don't you remember what you did to me in front of him!" I snap.

"Fuck all of that. I'm not trying to hear that shit. T, I can help you with your bills but what are you going to do for me?"

"What?" I question knowingly.

"Look I'm not giving away my money if I'm not getting anything back in return."

"You are some shit!"

"Tell me, what are you going to do?"

"When do you want me to come over nigga?" I ask not believing that I am degrading myself.

"Come over in an hour, my company should be gone."

"I will be there."

I know that Rashad is expecting for me to come over and give him some ass but that is not happening. I know that he has been with too many women and he doesn't deserve my body after continuing to treat me wrong. I know Rashad more than anyone and I know that he can't resist me. I plan on teasing him with my beauty and that will give me any amount of money that I desire.

I go into my closet and find my shortest jean shorts and the tightest T-shirt that I can find. I look in the mirror making sure that Rashad will be able to see my ass cheeks and nipples through the shirt. I wet my hair pulling it back into a pony tail so that I can show my face. I want to show him what he is missing.

A block from Rashad's house, I notice cars in

front. I continue to slow drive towards the house and I recognize Malik's car but not the other. I figure that Rashad has gone out and bought another car to show off for his bitches.

I park across the street and before I get out, I apply lip gloss for shine. I might tease him with a kiss so that he can taste the cherry lip gloss. Applying baby oil to my legs I look over and I notice the front door opening. My eyes are staring directly at the door anticipating for whomever to walk out.

I open my car door beginning to walk across the street but a car speeds by stopping me in my tracks. I quickly rush across the street having the sounds of my heels slap against the pavement.

The closer I get towards the driveway I become nervous. Suddenly Brandi steps out the house closing the door behind her. I look at her strangely and she just smiles pulling out the remote start for the car that I thought was Rashad's. I know this nigga didn't buy her a car and I am struggling to raise his kid? I say to myself.

Brandi climbs into the car without speaking to me. I stop and stare at her because I notice that she is wearing a pair of my heels that he had bought for me. I feel my blood pressure rising as I contemplate if I should run over there and beat her ass. Before pulling off she puts on a pair of Gucci frames and speeds off giving me the peace sign.

"You fucking bitch!" I shout as she zooms past.

I open the door without knocking or announcing

my presence. Rashad and Malik are fusing at each other over a video game. I notice that Rashad has taken down all of the pictures of us as a family but kept pictures of Raymond. He has even bought new furniture and a bigger size television. Rashad has taken out my plush furniture to put in a pool table.

"Excuse me."

Rashad looks over his shoulder, "T, wait this game is almost over."

"Boy, I have things to do."

"Like what?" he asks sarcastically.

"Like pay bills."

"T, since you are here get us some beers from the refrigerator."

I grab the two cold beers from the refrigerator placing them on the counter and I see my favorite bottle of wine. I decide to pour myself a glass and sip while he is playing his game.

"T, what's taking you so damn long to bring the beers? They are right there on the bottom shelf."

"I know where they are!" I shout walking towards them.

I place the bottles on a table in front of them but I purposely put my ass in Rashad's face for him to see my ass cheeks but my breast almost popped out of my shirt in front of Malik. I catch his eyes aimed on my breast as I stand up getting myself together.

"Rashad, can we talk about what I came over here for?"

"Malik hold up, let me talk to her for a minute."

Rashad pulls me into Raymond's old room slapping me on the ass as he cracks the door behind him. "How much do you need?"

"I need a lot." I answer looking at a wad of cash.

"I need a lot also."

"Maybe, later tonight. I have to pay these bills and get back to our son."

"How about, now?"

"No, not now. You know that we can't do nothing with your cousin out there."

"You can't give your husband some pussy but you can show mutherfucking strangers your shit before me."

"What are you talking about Rashad? I haven't shown anybody anything."

"So you are telling me that you wasn't stripping for them niggas?"

"Well." I say formulating a response.

Kenerly

"I know that you and your friend Brandi was shaking y'all ass for them niggas, T. Malik told me how you were bouncing your ass and having niggas feel all over you. You probably fucked one of them!"

"Yes I was dancing but I didn't let anyone touch me! Why are you trying to play me like I am a hoe? You know that I didn't fuck any of them lame ass niggas."

"Yes you did lying ass bitch!" Rashad barks slapping me in the face.

"I didn't fuck nobody!" I shout waving my hands in disgust.

"Well you are about to fuck me." Rashad says walking closer to me.

"No I'm not."

Rashad grabs me violently and attempts to pull off my shorts. I pull away from him slapping him multiple times in the face. He forcefully chokes me picking me up off the floor. I kick him hard in his nuts getting him to release his grasp. I turn for the door but he quickly snatches my shirt tearing it off my body. Before I have a chance to react he picks me up and throws me onto the bed.

"You are going to give me my pussy."

"Rashad stop." I plead.

Rashad ignores my plea and climbs on top of me forcing his weight down. He holds me down by the neck and uses his free hand to pull my shorts down my thighs.

105

"Rashad stop, baby please." I whine.

"Bitch shut the fuck up. You know that you want this dick. You like it rough."

He continues to tug at my panties until he is able to throw them across the room. I feel his dick becoming harder as he inches it closer to me. I frantically squirm trying to get away from this crazy man.

"Stop moving!"

"Why are you doing this to me?"

"This is what you want. You want to act like a hoe so I will treat you like one. I be damn if you give up my pussy to somebody without my permission, bitch."

"No!" I scream feeling his dick thrust inside me.
He finally let go of my neck and digs inside of me aggressively. I tightly close my eyes wishing he would stop. He holds me down by the waist to position himself for deeper penetration. I again hit him rapidly in his face but he continues to pound me.

I have become tired form all of the energy that I have used trying to resist, so I lay back and wait until he is satisfied. Rashad is sweating and breathing heavily as he rapidly works on top of me. My cries doesn't affect him any. Suddenly he comes inside me. I can feel every squirt being shot up in me.

When Rashad climbs off of me I notice Malik standing right behind him with that strange look on his face again. I quickly sit up reaching for my shorts but Rashad takes them from me.

"Come get you some, cuz." Rashad orders waving Malik over towards me.

I manage to get to my feet but Rashad wrestles me back to the bed. I look behind me and Malik is pulling down his pants. Rashad lays on my back while Malik squeeze his dick in-between my ass cheeks into my ass.

"You punk ass mutherfuckas!"

Malik forces his dick in my ass hurting me badly. Malik's dick is huge or at least it feels big going in back there. It does not take long for him to have an orgasm but he pulls out his dick shooting his juice over my back.
"Here's what you came here for." Rashad laughs dropping bills on me like I was stripping.

Rashad and Malik leave the room talking about what they have done to me. I am hurting from the inside out but I don't waste any time getting dress. I rapidly run out the house not looking at either one of them rushing to get inside my car.

On the way home I search through my phone for someone to talk to. Without having anyone else to call that I trust, I decide to call Brian because he is a great listener. He is shocked to hear from me knowing that I have put our relationship on hold. Brian teases me for not calling him, but he quickly takes notice that I am in a serious state of mind. Like a gentleman he apologizes and stresses to me that he is ready to listen.

Before giving him the details about what just

happened, I open myself up telling all of my secrets about my past. Brian is shocked to hear how I generate money but respects me for being honest.

"One day I will tell you about my old life and the silly shit I did before I got into the music business." Brian says understanding.

"So you do not look at me any different from the day we met?" I question waiting for a response.

"No. We all have a past. It's the lessons that you learn along the way."

Feeling a sense of comfort, I continue to tell him all of the events that led up to today. When I try to talk about the rape, I let out a loud cry and tears flood inside my hands. Brian gives me the courage to continue but he is unable to swallow my words easy. Brian becomes furious and wants to hurt Rashad and Malik himself. He cannot believe that a man that I have a child with, would do me like this after all I have done for him.

"Have you called the police yet and filed charges on them?"

"No. I have a crazy ass brother that will handle him for me. My brother has been itching to get him."

"Well if you need me to make a phone call, I will make sure that he won't ever hurt you or any other woman again."

"Thank you but I got this one, boo. I will call you later I have to get myself together." I say ending the call.

Kenerly

When I enter my apartment I dart to the bathroom to look at my bruises. Rashad has busted my lip and put a bruise on my face. I open my legs and see scratches and bruises all over my thighs from him grabbing me. The thought of nasty ass Malik's dick inside me has my chest becoming tight with anxiety. I climb into the shower making sure that it is hot enough to kill the germs on my body. I scrub myself so hard with my wash cloth that my whole body becomes red.

I get out of the shower thinking about everyone who has done me wrong whom I trusted. Out of all of them I would not have believed that Brandi would turn on me like a complete stranger.

"I have something for her ass," I say out loud.

I call Brandi and talk to her about the rape like nothing has changed between us. She acts as if she is really pissed and concerned about my welfare.

Brandi and I talk on the phone for hours trying to work out our friendship. I tell her that I would like for us to be together but we will have to take our time. Brandi is all for it, eating this dream up. I have her in the palm of my hands, so knowing how greedy she is, I tell her about Rashad's upcoming trip to buy some more drugs. This will be the perfect opportunity to get all of what I am owed. Brandi is down for my plan and for us to pay him back together.

After talking to Brandi, I call my brother for his help. Of course he wants to do some crazy shit to Rashad that only happens in horror movies but I calm him down telling him my plan. I only ask for him to watch my back if I slip or choke up. I know that Rashad is the father of my child but he sure don't act as if is. I know that I will become nervous when I do what I have done to many men before him. Lamar tells me that he wants me to take a gun with me just in case Rashad figures out my sting. I tell him that I will take his advice because I wasn't going to be hurt again by that man.

CHAPTER 13

One week later

Today Rashad is getting his money ready for the trip down to Atlanta. I choose today to do what I have planned knowing that he will be taking a lot of money with him and I want to catch him before he leaves.

"Rashad are you busy?" I ask in a soft tone calling him.

"Not right now. I am waiting for Malik to bring his slow ass over here so we can leave." He answers.

"I am wondering if I can get about five hundred dollars to buy Raymond a few outfits and some shoes."

"T, I really don't have it to give. You know that I have a lot of money tied into this shit."

"Rashad he really needs some new clothes. I know that you are not going to have your son wearing the same shit every day."

"Why can't you buy him some clothes?"

"I don't have the money."

"Can you wait until I come back? I have some money out in the streets that I will give to you."

"I'm not going for that. I know that you have some money to trick off to your little bitches."

"I just might. T, if you want the money I'm going to want something in return."

"What Rashad?"

"I want you to come over here and give me some of that good ass pussy." Rashad answers.

"Are you serious?"

"Yes I am."

"Can we do it like we did in Atlanta?" I ask.

"Hell yeah! Do you need me to call somebody?"

"What! There you go again playing me like I am a hoe. I am cool."

"No. No. No. T, I was not thinking that. Who do you have in mind?"

"I was thinking of asking Brandi since I know that you are fucking her anyway."

"Oh, Brandi. I will enjoy that."

"Really?" I say acting joyful.

"Try to get over in the next hour. I will call Malik and tell him to take his time."

"Where is he at because I don't want to see him."

"He is probably at home fucking his girl when

his ass needs to be out getting that money."

"All right I will see you soon." I say ending the call.

"Lamar, Rashad will be home for another hour but Malik is at home now. I am sure that he has his money there with him. Try to get over there before he leaves to round up some more money."

"Okay Treasure, I will handle that little nigga. You be safe and call me if you need any help."

"Thanks brother but I got this." I say hugging Lamar as he walks out my apartment.

I run into my bedroom opening my dresser finding my sexiest pair of thongs to put on. I pull the thongs on and quickly lotion my ass making sure that it looks good for Rashad. Checking myself in the mirror, I shake my ass to see how good it looks and it looks damn good.

Struggling to pull these tight jeans over my ass, I remember that I have to call Brandi. I pick up my phone and notice that I have been trying to get dressed for twenty minutes.

"Hello." Brandi answers.

"Girl, are you really wanting to do this?" I ask Brandi playing things off as if I am nervous.

"Hell yeah! If I were you, I would do more." Brandi responds.

"Have you talked to him yet?" I ask finally

pulling my pants up.

"Yeah about ten minutes ago. That fool don't know what he has coming. I think that we can do shit like this all of the time."

"It's not easy all of the time."

"Well it's better than shaking my ass for a bunch of strangers for pennies when I can get a baller for everything."

"Girl you are crazy. You are not ready for the shit I do." I laugh.

"Treasure I will prove it to you tonight."

"I hear you."

"I am pulling in his driveway now. Have you left the house yet?"

"I am walking out now." I say locking the door behind me.
"Okay, bye baby." Brandi says ending the call.

I climb in the car heading towards Rashad's house. While I am driving I am thinking about the last time that I was over there. Rashad deserves everything that he has coming to him.

Arriving at his house, I knock softly on the door. Brandi opens the door already dressed and ready.

"Hey, girl." Brandi says smiling from ear to ear.

"I see that you are ready." I say smiling back giving her the perception that I am happy to see her.

"Yes I am."

"Where is Rashad?" I ask looking around.

"He is in his room putting away his bags. I saw him grab two bags by the door when I came in." Brandi answers pointing towards the bedroom.

"Well let's go say hi." I say taking Brandi's hand and rushing towards the bedroom.gone

When we enter the bedroom, I notice that Rashad has gone all out. He has candles lit, slow music playing, and a bottle of wine with three glasses on the nightstand.

Rashad walks out of the walk-in closet looking sexy as ever. Wearing nothing but a pair of boxer briefs, I cannot help but to look at his package. He steps closer to us staring me in the eye. I wonder what is on his mind.

"Damn you look good T." Rashad charms.

"Thank you."

"How about you come out of them clothes and allow me to take care of that body." Rashad says smoothly.

"You just lay down we will take care of you." Brandi interjects.

Rashad walks over to the bed and opens the bottle. I watch him carefully pouring the wine in each glass.

I turn my back at him to take off my clothes and when I get down to my panties Brandi gives me a hard slap on the ass.

"That's what I'm talking about!" Rashad cheerfully shouts rubbing his hands together.

I turn back to Brandi and give her a passionate kiss to start the show. Brandi grabs onto my ass squeezing it tightly. When we separate she places my breast in her mouth and begins to suck. I feel her hands glide down my thighs and on my pussy. She rubs my pussy rapidly before putting her hands inside of my panties.

From my peripheral vision I see Rashad pulling down his boxers and touching himself. Brandi pulls me toward the bed. I fall back on the bed and she quickly straddles me.

Brandi goes down on me sliding my panties aside to taste my sweat nectar. Brandi is unable to get into it because Rashad sits up trying to touch on her.

"Come on girl let's give this man some attention." Brandi says irritated.

Brandi crawls over to Rashad and sticks his dick deep down her throat without gagging. I can tell that she has sucked his dick many times by the way she is working her tongue over his shaft. Rashad grabs her by the hair and guides her as she goes to work. I take this opportunity to climb off the bed and take off my panties. Rashad is staring at me hard. I tease him by licking my lips.

I pull Brandi off of him and we put on a seductive show tasting one another for him in a sixty-nine position.

Rashad lyes on the bed watching us, becoming excited. I wave for him to join us and he quickly puts on a condom. I allow him to fuck Brandi as I play with myself.

Rashad keeps eye contact with me as he fucks her until he comes. He closes his eyes tightly and releases his juices. Brandi holds his head down to her breast and continues to work her ass until she has an orgasm.

Rashad gets up feeling himself like he is big and bad. He walks towards me stroking his dick trying to get it hard again.

"Now it's your turn." He says continuing to touch himself.

"No we have one more thing for you before we get real nasty. I want you to lye on the bed and get ready for the ride of your life." I say grabbing Brandi's arm wanting her to get next to me.

"You bitches need to hurry up. I don't have all day." Rashad says flopping back down on the bed.

Brandi and I step away from Rashad so that I can tell her what I have in mind.

"Brandi, I want you to ride the hell out of his muthafucking dick for me. While you are fucking him I will take the bags of money from the closet." I instruct.

"Okay. I got you, baby." Brandi says kissing me and hopping to the bed.

Soon as she straddles Rashad and let out a

sensual moan, I rush into the closet. I look insides both bags making sure that I am taking the money. Checking the bags I am satisfied seeing all of the stacks of cash.

Walking out of the closet all I can see is Brandi's ass in the air bouncing on his shaft. I quickly grab my clothes and get dressed.

"Where are you going?" Rashad asks catching me off guard as I try to sneak out of the room.

"I have to go."

"Shit! Like hell you think your leaving with my money!" Rashad shouts throwing Brandi off him.

Rashad jumps out of the bed and rapidly walks towards me. I throw a bag off of my shoulder and dig in my purse pulling out the pistol Lamar gave me.

"Oh shit!" Rashad shouts being stopped in his tracks.

"Yeah nigga you remember this?" I ask aiming the gun at his chest.

"T, baby. Baby please don't shoot me." Rashad pleads.

"Nigga you and your bitch ass cousin raped me! Your sorry ass deserves to die."

"T shoot his ass!" Brandi orders.

I look at the two of them and become sick to the

stomach. Just thinking of her going behind my back and fucking my husband has me fired up.

"Brandi, do you still want to be together?" I ask.

"Why you ask me that? Brandi questions, trying to hurry to get dress.

"Do you love me?" I ask raising my voice louder.

"Yes I do." She says pulling up her pants.
"Prove it." I say pointing at Rashad.

"Prove it?" Branding questions narrowing her eyes at me.

"This man has taken everything from me. He has raped me and has hurt his son. Now if you say you love me then prove it." I stress.

Brandi walks over to me taking the gun from my hand.

"Brandi, come on now. Please don't do this. How much do you want?" Rashad pleads.

She points the gun directly at Rashad. Boom! Boom! Boom! Brandi shoots ripping his body up with bullets.

I tell Brandi to put the gun away while I go into the bathroom and clean myself up. Inside the bathroom I call Lamar.

"Brandi did it for me bro." I whisper into the

phone.

"Okay leave the house now. The police will be arriving soon." Lamar orders.

"Did you take care of my other problem?"

"You know that I did. I put that problem to bed." Lamar answers.
"Alright I will see you later." I say ending the call.

When I walk in the bedroom Brandi is shaken. She is standing shaking uncontrollably looking over Rashad's lifeless body.

"Brandi get yourself together, we need to make this house look as if someone was trying to rob him."

"I shot him T. Is he dead?"

"Yes he's gone. Where did you put the gun?" I ask grabbing her by the shoulders.

"It's in my purse." Brandi answers.

"Okay tear this room up. I will tear up down stairs."

Brandi begins to pull clothes down in the closet and tossing clothes on the floor. I leave the room with the bags heading for my car. I can hear the police sirens coming closer. Quickly I throw the bags in the trunk and open the driver's door taking a seat.

Suddenly four cruisers pull up and all of the police men rush inside. Within a few moments, I hear more gun shots being fired. I become so scared that I call Brian.

"Brian I need you to come get me." I say anxiously.

"Where are you?"

"It's complicated. I don't even know why I am calling you." I say as tears flow down my face.

"Whatever it is, I am here for you. I need you to calm down and tell me what's wrong." Brian says sincerely.

"My best friend killed my husband. I don't know what to do."

"Damn Treasure, that is fucked up."

"I. I am so sorry that I called you Brian." I stutter.

"No don't be. Treasure you can always call me for anything."

"I have to go Brian."

"You don't want me to come and get you now?" he asks sounding very concerned.

"No, I will be fine. I have to go." I hang the phone up on him. I wipe away my tears and climb out the car slowly moving towards the front door. Two officers stop me at the door.

"You can't go in there!" An officer shouts.

"This is my house!" I shout making myself cry.

About five minutes later the crime scene and coroner's office shows up. I am wondering if they are going to arrest me. My phone begins to vibrate and when I look at it I have received a message from Brian telling me that he is worried .

A detective asks me to sit on the couch so that he can ask me some questions. I answer all of his questions allowing him to draw his w conclusion. The detective believes that Rashad and Brandi were having an affair and she shot him because he wouldn't leave me. I go right along with it because his story was not far from the truth.

Watching both of their bodies being carried out on stretchers, I break down in tears. The detective tells me that I can go and if he has any other questions he would like to call me. I give him my phone number and leave the house.

Outside the house there is a crowd of spectators. I notice a few of my neighbors watching me very carefully, so I force myself to cry before climbing into my car.

I rush out of the neighborhood without any direction. After all of this madness, all I want is to be love. I pull up in Brian's driveway wondering if he is going to let me in after the way I have been playing him.

Getting out of the car I notice how nervous I have become. My legs are shaking, but I continue to walk up the stone steps towards the door.

I ring the door-bell, patiently waiting for Brian to answer, but after a few moments I begin to walk back down the steps.

"Where are you going?" Brian asks.

I turn around so fast amazed to see him at the door. "Brian."

"You don't have to explain anything. It's good to see you, Treasure."

"It's good to see you too." I say running into his arms.

Brian picks me up and takes me into his bedroom where he has set the mood. I figure that this is the reason why he was taking a while to answer the door. He gently places me down on his pillow-top bed and begins to apply kisses all over my body. Each kiss sends chills over my body. I am anxious for him to come inside of me but he takes his time. Brian makes sure that I am completely relaxed before entering me.

"Damn Treasure."

"It's all yours." I say feeling safe in his arms.

ABOUT THE AUTHOR

SHAUNTA KENERLY, was born in Springfield, Ohio but raised in Dayton, Ohio. He found his love with writing fiction while incarcerated. After being released he continued to write novels and short stories from his own experiences and real life experiences from what he sees in our community. The passion he has for writing is clearly proven through his characters and story line. His characters convince you that you are either one of them or you know the characters. Shaunta continues to write, in which he hopes to be a voice for his community and a positive role model for young men.

COMING OCTOBER 3RD

"CAN'T TRUST HER, CAN'T TRUST HIM..."

SHAUNTA KENERLY

WITH

ANDREA HIBBLER

CHAPTER 1
ANTHONY

"Damn it feels good to be getting out of this hell hole today." I say tearing the linen off my bunk bed and throwing my dirty state blues onto the floor. I had one of the laundry guys steal me a new state uniform from the laundry room so that I can look fresh before I jumped into some real clothes that my girl, Angel bought for me. Knowing how I am, she ordered me a pair of Nike's last week to step out in. I already had a pair but I usually wear them when she comes to visit. I gave these pair away along with new socks and T-shirts to my niggas who I knew, that wouldn't be coming home anytime soon. I want to be all the way clean, leaving all of this bullshit behind me and trying to make a real legitimate life for myself. Being incarcerated for six years has changed a lot about me. Coming in, I was a twenty-four year old knuckle head and now I am a thirty year old grown man.

I was watching some old friends of mine play chess in the yard yesterday. They are so close to me that I consider them family. They asked me what was I really going to do once I got out. A lot of niggas are talking shit, basically. They are talking about how much they have changed simply because they have found religion. Others talk tough. They are talking as if they would just do the same things that landed them in here to begin with. I never talk much about my case because I never know who I can trust or who is really listening. However, the streets talk and my friends know that I am in here for drug trafficking, but do not know the details of my case.

Six years ago, Angel and I were moving a lot of dope on the highway from our home in Hampton, Virginia to my

126

home state of Ohio. Angel being mixed with two different ethnicities, Columbian and Black, she was able to relate with the Latin and Spanish dealers who would not do any business with just me. I was only buying half bricks of heroin when I met Angel. Angel was selling cocaine to my uncle, who was the one that brought me here in order to get away from my crazy life back home. I had seen the quality of the cocaine product and sales were great so I had to introduce myself to her. I showed her my character by giving her my savings to buy two bricks of heroin, not knowing if she would ever return. She was taken off guard by my actions and promised to return with my order. The very next day Angel called me and we met up to get my shit. Angel was very much connected through her family and took me out of the dope houses into a half million dollar home. This also meant access to an unlimited amount of dope. Unfortunately, after three years of hustling together, an informant gave up information on Angel.

Angel and I decided to meet up with the informant at the usual spot and the police jumped out on us. I was stunned to see how much work the police put into capturing us. Detectives found two bricks of cocaine in the car and both of our guns. Angel's face said it all to me. She was scared to death of going behind bars. I had spent a year behind bars before on a drug possession charge. I had to eat this charge for her not knowing what would happen to her behind bars. I loved her enough to take the charge. My main concern was that I did not want her taking down the whole organization in fear of the anticipated interrogation in the near future.

I was upset with her because I told her that I did not want to do business with the informant anymore. It was because I was getting a funny feeling about him. He started to ask questions about pricing for future weight. There would be differences with his price as if he had hooked us up with some other people looking to buy. Just before we left the stash house, I told her how I was feeling about him and now we were staring at each other in the back seat of two separate unmarked police cruisers. I pounded my fist against my forehead knowing that I should have trusted my gut feeling. Angel cried telling me that she was sorry, knowing why I was so upset. I told her not to say a word to the police and signaled with my hand for her to call my uncle and tell him about the situation. I was hoping that he would come down to the county jail to bail me out before my court date. I was told that it is best to go in front of the judge dressed like I am a serious business man in a suit rather than coming in with chains on and a jail jumper.

Arriving at the county jail, I made the detective's job really easy by admitting to everything. Taking these charges was harder than I thought. Besides that, the rule is to never admit to anything even if the police found the product in your pocket. The detectives told me the amount of time that I would be facing if I take the charges, but I brushed them off with scare tactics. One of them basically told me that he didn't want me. However, what they really wanted was any contacts or connections I had knowledge of. I sat down reminding myself in my head to keep quiet and prepare myself for the worst.

I waited four months for my uncle to bail me out but he never came. After a few weeks he, stopped answering my calls. The only way I was able to make contact, was when Angel went over to his house to drop off his work. Angel continued to answer my calls, but when I went up before the judge for sentencing, I stood all alone listening to my plea agreement.

CHAPTER 2

"Adams! Anthony Adams! Pack your shit!" Officer MacLean shouts down the corridor.

I am so glad that this will be the last time I hear his nagging voice. We have had our words but today I will have the last laugh leaving this bitch. I stand over him waiting for him to say something smart. I made the most of my time in here. I basically lived in the weight room or outside on the bars. I am now a solid rock at 240 pounds barely displaying any body fat. Actually I wish that he would say something, because my first inclination is to follow him to his house and beat him down. I stand there thinking this to myself.

I can hear cheers from the inmates wishing me good luck as I walk toward the door. I always wondered what this day would feel like. I have seen so many come in and just as many come right back. Because my arms were full of boxes containing letters and personal items, I am unable to waive goodbye. I just turn around and nod, letting everyone know that I heard them.

After receiving my state identification picture, I am allowed to leave. Opening the door, I look all around the visitation room for Angel, but to my dismay she was not there. I place my items down and head for the exit staring out towards the parking lot.

"Fuck!" I shout receiving the attention of a female officer.

Last night when we were talking, I asked her to be up here around 9 A.M. knowing that they would not release me on time. I look up at the clock and it is 9:45 and she is not here yet. I told her last night that I did not want to wait around. I was starting to believe that she is still in the bed, due to our long conversation last night. I must have called her at least ten times. I knew the phone bill was sky high. I slowly walk toward the phones and Angel surprises me out of nowhere, running to me with open arms. I lift her up high and hug her as tight as I can. I gently place her down giving her a deep passionate kiss, as if we were getting married. When we separate, I take a step back to take notice of her body. She is wearing some fitted jeans and a tight shirt revealing her golden breast.

"Oh I missed you," she blushes.

"I missed you too baby. Now let's get the fuck away from here." I say, quickly walking towards the main exit.

Driving to the house, her phone constantly keeps ringing. I try to ignore the phone calls and the fact that she is talking in codes to multiple callers, but now it has become a problem. The next time the phone rang I stop her from answering and ask her about the repeated calls. I am thinking she has some nigga waiting for her. I honestly would not be upset if she did have a man while I was locked up, but I feel like it is time for that shit to end.

"Nobody that you need to be worried about," she answers staring ahead.

"Okay Angel. I am home now."

"Boy, everybody knows that you are home. Chill out

Poppi."

Our conversation isn't what I expected coming home. Something about her is different and I am determined to figure it out.

Pulling up to the house, I notice that she has maintained the landscape to my liking. We climb out of the car and she orders me to go directly to the bedroom. I laugh at her excitement but I have been anticipating this moment for a long time. I rush inside the house and wait for her to enter. Angel stands outside arguing with someone on the phone. I walk through the house and notice that she has made some changes. As a matter of fact, she changed a lot of shit. It is as if she had a home makeover crew come in and go wild.

Angel walks in smiling from ear to ear showing all of her pretty whites. She simply acts as if I'm not going to notice the changes she   made to the house without telling me. That information would have been good to read in a letter from her, or at least have something to discuss during a visit before the changes were made.

I attempt to share what is on my mind about the changes, but before I can say a word, she jumps on me wrapping her legs around my waist. Angel quickly steals a kiss from me and I do not hesitate to give in. We share another passionate kiss, swirling each others tongue across each other's. I grab her ass and squeeze it tightly, reenacting the fantasy I had in my sleep on the inside. Her butt was so soft that it is causing my manhood to become erect. She notices my bulge against her and tells me that it is time for her to handle her business. I gently place her down and before I could blink my eyes she is on her knees taking all of me in her mouth.

"Damn girl, you did miss me." I said this in a low tone while enjoying the movements of her tongue swirl over my shaft.

"Yes I did P," she says pausing for a brief moment and then goes back to pleasing me.

I know that she does not like for me to have an orgasm in her mouth, so I pull myself away and proceed to take her to the couch. I bend her over and slowly remove her pants while simultaneously kissing on her backside. I am surprised to see that she is not wearing any panties and I was delighted. Finally getting her pants off, I position myself behind her and take my time easing in. Angel is so wet inside which causes me to become that much more excited and thrust a little harder. Angel doesn't allow me to take control and begins to throw her ass at me. I take notice that she has added some new movements to this position.

Angel continues to bounce her ass against my thighs taking every inch of me until I lose total control and explode inside of her. Normally she would have hopped off me quick and begin to talk shit, but this time she did not speak a word. Feeling as if I had to prove myself to her, I pick her up and walk to the bedroom with intentions of making passionate love.